WHEN SHE ESCAPED

A THRILLER

JENIFER RUFF

Greyt Companion Press

WHEN SHE ESCAPED
A THRILLER

Copyright © 2025 Greyt Companion Press

ISBN ebook: 978-1-954447-36-3

ISBN paperback: 978-1-954447-37-0

ISBN hardback: 978-1-954447-38-7

Written by Jenifer Ruff

Cover design by Damonza

PART 1

ZIPPORAH

CHAPTER 1

Hannah Williams is going to die. I have to kill her. Raven's Hollow Resort is where I'll make it happen.

Standing at the resort's entrance, the crisp mountain air brings on a touch of lightheaded excitement. The resort is a beautiful, peaceful place to write, and I have ten days to complete a rough draft of my new book.

I keep my sunglasses and wide-brimmed hat on to protect my privacy as I enter the lobby. I'm greeted with wooden beams, a stone fireplace, and rustic decorations. A young woman staffs the check-in desk, wearing a black uniform with the resort's raven logo.

"Reservation for Hannah Williams," I say, though it's not my real name. Hannah Williams is the protagonist in my latest thriller novel. She's the unfortunate soul who won't be alive when my book ends. Donna, my editor, is waiting on standby for my first few chapters. Based on what I've told her, she's especially excited about this book. She's also the person who recommended Raven's Hollow.

The young woman at the check-in desk is typing when a man in the same uniform appears beside her. Over her shoulder, his gaze drops to the tablet in her hands. Then he looks up at me and smiles.

"Welcome, Ms. Williams. I'm Gerald, the general manager. If you need anything during your stay, please let us assist."

"Thank you. I appreciate that," I say. Then paranoia hits me. I hope he's not aware of my real identity. I've tried to maintain a low profile throughout my career. There are no photos of me on my book jackets or website. I rarely speak in public, and I avoid social media. I'm probably overreacting now, and the manager treats all guests the same. I worry anyway. I don't want any distractions while I'm here.

"If you're planning on booking any spa appointments, please schedule them early in your stay. Those appointments fill up fast," he tells me.

I'm less anxious, thanks to his comment. He'd ensure me a spot if he recognized me.

He hands me my room key and a glossy resort map as an outdoorsy young man transfers my luggage onto a brass cart. I follow him out of the lodge and onto a paved path, looking for details to enhance the story still forming in my head. Is there anything peculiar about the resort, or even the young man, that I could include in my novel?

"How long have you worked here?" I ask.

Without slowing, he turns to me. "Just two months. I'm a student at the University of Colorado. A business major. This is my summer job."

I grin. "I can think of far worse places to spend a summer."

"You're right, but you've got to see this place in the winter. That's my favorite season here. The skiing is the best."

I attempt to picture everything covered in a thick blanket of snow. It might be pretty, but I'm not a fan of cold temperatures. I prefer June and the near-perfect seventy-three degrees we have today. Just thinking about the snow makes me uneasy.

As we head through the heart of the resort to the guest wings, we pass the ski lodge and equipment rental area. Beyond those are restaurants, a spa, a fitness center and pool, and a charming café. Before my arrival, I explored the resort's website. I'm familiar with the menus and activities. Now that I'm here, the place doesn't disappoint. If I get married someday, I'd want the wedding somewhere like this, with gorgeous views. Ironically, the novel I plan to draft here will be dramatically different from my surroundings. I'm going to create a world more like hell than a mountain paradise.

The bellhop guides us past a stone firepit ringed with Adirondack chairs, and I remember from my research that the resort provides complimentary ingredients for s'mores. I picture guests gathered around the firepits at night, their faces illuminated by the flickering flames, marshmallow sticks hovering close to the heat while they share stories.

After a gradual climb, we finally reach the building where I'll be staying. Elk Lodge stands atop a hill, and from this vantage point, I'm aware of how secluded we are. An endless wilderness surrounds us, separating the resort from the rest of the world.

The young man places my bags in my room, and I give him a generous tip.

My suite is a fabulous mix of mountain decor with natural elements and modern comforts. I plan to have a luxurious soak in the large claw-foot tub. Before unpacking a single item, I take photos from every angle to capture the cozy, rustic ambiance.

The king-size bed looks comfortable, though too big for one person. It reminds me I've been without a romantic partner for quite some time. I'm wary of letting anyone get too close.

Tugging on a metal chain, I pull heavy layers of curtains open, revealing a balcony with sliding glass doors. The early afternoon sun streams in, and the view framed by my window is magnificent. This will do. I snap a few more photos, so I'll have something to remember after I've left.

With a few more things left to do before I settle in, I open the mini-fridge and grab a bottle of water. The resort is 8,500 feet above sea level, and hydration prevents altitude sickness. I've suffered from altitude before. There's nothing fun about being sick and woozy. It's even caused me to hallucinate in the past.

Rather than unpack the suitcase with my clothes, I unzip the carry-on containing all my writing tools. I get my laptop situated on the desk where I can take in the incredible views and set my wireless mouse beside it.

Last, I put some of my novels on the shelf above the dresser. The novels bear my real name—Zipporah Bazile. As my mother used to say, the Z is pronounced soft, as in breeze. Zi-pho-rah. Same with the z in Bazile.

I write dark psychological thrillers with unexpected twists. The titles I brought with me—*Her Darkest Lies, Her Darkest Dilemma, Her Darkest Fears*—represent three of the thirty books in my *Darkness* series. I'm fascinated with revealing the dark side hiding within otherwise normal people, and I usually contrast that with the gritty, selfless bravery of my beloved protagonist.

Behind my desk, I scoot from side to side, getting comfortable in the stately leather chair. The beauty on the other side of my windows will disappear when I unleash my imagination and focus on the disturbing tale waiting for me there.

My new manuscript starts with Hannah and the pivotal moment before her life falls apart.

CHAPTER 2

Hannah pulled her coat on, ready to exit the Tesla when Jackson stopped at the highway rest area. Thanks to the coffee she'd consumed, she was desperate. Even before he switched the vehicle into park, she jumped out, clutching her purse, leaving her phone charging on the console.

Frosty clouds of breath escaped her lips as she hurried through the darkness to the bathrooms, zipping her coat up. One lamp was broken, and another cast a flickering shadow on the asphalt path. Hannah glanced back at Jackson. The car's interior light illuminated him in the driver's seat, mouth moving, earbuds in his ears. She hoped his work issues wouldn't dominate their weekend and ruin the romantic getaway she'd planned. She'd been looking forward to it for over two months. Already, his last-minute work emergency had cost them an entire evening. They left the city after 10 p.m., five hours later than planned.

Rather than getting irritated, Hannah shifted her sympathy to Jackson. Thanks to an unexpected work crisis, his day wasn't going well. She'd booked this peaceful mountain retreat so they could relax together and escape the stress of their jobs for three days. Her laptop was in her suitcase in the car, but she wasn't planning on doing any editing work during their trip.

When she returned to the car, she could suggest they forgo the trip and head back to Charlotte. Jackson could work from his corporate office until his crisis blew over, and she could schedule the cabin getaway for another long weekend. It wouldn't be the first occasion where she'd put someone else's needs above hers. She would at least broach the subject to gauge his response.

Three doors marked *restroom* awaited her. Hannah went for the first, a single room with yellowish light and a dingy cement floor. She'd been in there a minute when someone knocked on the door.

"Jackson?" she asked.

When no one responded, Hannah said, "I'm in here. Just a minute."

She frowned, realizing there was no toilet paper. Perhaps the other restrooms didn't have paper either, and that's why someone was waiting on this one. She rummaged through her purse for a tissue and found an unopened travel pack tucked into a side pocket. She removed two sheets for herself, and left the rest of the tissues for the next people.

Mindful of someone waiting, she hurriedly washed her hands with cold water. With no paper towels or air dryer to dry her hands, she shook them out. Eager to get back in the warm car, she twisted the bolt and opened the door.

Before she could scream, a massive hand clamped over her mouth, and an arm that felt like solid muscle yanked her close.

Hannah fought against a man's vice-like grip, her body writhing, her limbs kicking and flailing. A sharp pinch pierced her neck, causing an even stronger bolt of terror. She twisted enough to see the Tesla in the distance. The interior light was off, concealing Jackson behind the windshield. Could he see her? Was he aware of what was happening?

Those were her last thoughts before blackness descended.

CHAPTER 3

FROM THE MANUSCRIPT

Jackson glanced through the windshield just in time to see Hannah enter the restroom.

"I understand, Mr. Orinthorpe," Jackson said. "Please bear with us while we resolve the issue."

Mr. Orinthorpe huffed loudly. "This is costing me a small fortune. I need this fixed now, not later!"

"When I get off the phone with you, I'll check with our IT team again to see if they've come up with a solution." Jackson scrolled through his texts, hoping for a positive update on the debacle.

"Every passing minute is affecting my business. I expect better from your bank," Mr. Orinthorpe said.

"I understand, and again, I apologize. I'll keep you updated on our progress," Jackson said, realizing he'd just committed to ruining the weekend Hannah had planned.

"Hold on," Mr. Orinthorpe snapped. "Don't go anywhere. I've got to check on something."

Jackson peered through the front window, expecting to see Hannah. He strummed his fingers over the steering wheel. What was taking her so long? Was she sick? Did she stop to talk with someone? He looked around. There were no other vehicles in sight. The rest stop was empty.

He checked the time display on the car's center screen. Fifteen minutes had slipped away since she entered the restroom. Frowning, he stared out the window again, annoyance mingling with impatience. He had to get online and back to work as soon as they arrived at the rental cabin, and he hoped the internet strength was sufficient. A long night awaited him, and he regretted leaving the office. He thought his team finally had the situation under control. He was mistaken.

Orinthorpe hadn't returned to the line, so Jackson put the call on mute and got out of his car, leaving his coat behind in the back seat. Wincing in the cold, he jogged toward the restrooms. He knocked on the first door, only to be met with silence. Walking down the line, he repeated the process. Moving in the opposite direction, he opened each door and found all the rooms and stalls empty.

"Jackson. Did you hear my question?" Orinthorpe asked.

"Can you say that again?" Jackson forgot to take his phone off mute and had to repeat himself.

"I said nothing has changed on my end. I'm this close to taking all my business elsewhere and suing you. Tell me again what you're doing to fix this."

"Everything we can. Give me a minute. I'll be right back," Jackson said before pushing mute again.

"Hannah!" he shouted, scanning the rest area.

Had she mentioned a walk to stretch her legs, and he hadn't heard? But would she walk by herself in the dark?

Leaving the bathrooms, he walked the path encircling the entire rest area. He saw no one and heard nothing beyond the whooshing of speeding traffic on the highway.

Was this Hannah's way of getting back at him because he'd been on the phone since leaving the city? Except that wasn't at all like Hannah. She didn't play petty games. Throughout their two-year relationship, she'd been nothing but understanding and supportive of his crazy work hours. Of course, it helped that her father was the CFO at a large bank. Hannah knew long hours and unexpected crises came with top positions, or in Jackson's case, working your way toward one.

"Hannah! Where are you?" he shouted.

There was no sign of her.

Potential scenarios played out in Jackson's mind, each more disturbing than the last.

He took his phone off mute, said, "I have to call you back," and hung up without waiting for a response.

Stuffing his earbuds into his pocket, Jackson scanned the area again. He wrapped his arms around his body and turned in a slow circle, peering into the darkness. "Hannah!" he screamed at the top of his lungs. "Hannah!"

As his panic escalated, he broke into a run, venturing partway down the on-ramp, bellowing Hannah's name into the night. His cries went unanswered. This couldn't be happening. She couldn't have just vanished. There had to be an explanation, a logical reason for her absence.

Mind racing with confusion, Jackson jogged back to his car. Hannah's suitcase remained, but her purse and coat were gone. That gave him an instant of hope until he spotted her iPhone attached to a charger. She'd never leave it behind.

Something was wrong.

He dropped his head into his hands to think. His phone rang. Mr. Orinthorpe again. Jackson ignored it, grabbed his coat, and retraced his steps around the area. He scoured every hiding place—the bathrooms, behind the vending machines, even lifting the covers of the giant trash bins until there was nowhere else to look.

Hannah was gone.

I've reached an excellent stopping place in my novel. Four uninterrupted hours passed in the blink of an eye. I'd remained glued to my seat, trying to channel fear and helplessness. It's nice to let go of that intensity now. I push my chair back and stretch, rolling my head from side to side.

Just like my editor, I'm excited about where this story will go next.

Now it's time to explore the resort.

CHAPTER 4

In the corridor outside my hotel room, I unfold the resort map and locate Raven's Watch Tavern, the resort's fine dining restaurant with locally sourced food. It's late for dinner, for me at least. Time slipped away while I wrote. The sun set an hour ago, and there's a chill in the air as I follow the signage leading to the restaurant.

As I walk, I sense someone just a few strides behind me. A quick turn reveals a man wearing a dark-colored dress shirt and slacks. He's approximately my age and attractive. I don't turn around again until I get to Raven's Watch Tavern, but I can hear his footsteps.

At the host stand, he waits a respectful distance from me. While he's looking at his phone, I sneak a longer look, long enough to notice his expressive brown eyes and to confirm that he's a good-looking guy.

The hostess returns to her post, gathers menus, and asks, "Two of you dining with us tonight?"

We respond at the same time with, "Just one" and "We're not together."

The hostess leads me through the candle-lit restaurant first. A massive stone fireplace dominates the center of the room, reaching up to the wood-beamed ceiling. The hearth is open on two sides, with a cozy fire burning. The tables nearest are all occupied. I make a mental note to arrive early tomorrow and snag one of those coveted spots.

At my table, I look up from reading my menu as the hostess passes me again. She leads the handsome man to a table not far from mine. He takes a seat facing me. Rather than staring straight at him, I gaze toward the elderly couple speaking French to my right and then to the much younger couple holding hands across the table to my left.

I order wine and a main course—the Wagyu beef tenderloin with whipped potatoes and grilled asparagus—but decline the breadbasket my server brings. When my entrée arrives, the presentation is so fabulous that I immortalize it with a photo of my plate. I'll keep the image private, rather than share where I am or what I'm doing. It's just for me. The next time I describe a beautiful meal in one of my novels, I might consult this picture to help me with the details.

I hadn't realized how hungry I was until I take the first bite. The food is amazing.

I'm sipping a wonderful Cabernet when a server delivers a plate to the man nearby. It's the same meal I ordered. I can't help wondering who he is and why he's here alone. He doesn't wear a wedding band, but that doesn't count for much. He might have a significant other waiting in his room, not in the mood for dinner because of altitude sickness.

As we eat at our separate tables, my thoughts drift back to my novel. I wrote and revised close to two thousand words today, which is a great start.

An idea for the next chapter pops into my head. I picture Hannah waking up terrified in the back of her abductor's van. While plotting my novel, I steal glances at the man seated nearby. We're both finished with our meals. When the server delivers our bills in succession, we rise from our tables and end up walking out together.

"Seems we're well synced," the man says, sounding amused.

My better judgment tells me to smile politely and say goodnight, but a reckless impulse stirs inside me. "I was thinking of having a nightcap."

His eyes light up. "I'd like that. If you're open to company?"

"I am. Though I should mention it's my first day here, and I have no idea where I'm going."

"Second day for me," he says, "I'm headed to The Summit Bar. I know the way, which tells you where I went last night after dinner." He laughs, his voice deep and warm, and I catch the clean scent of his cologne or aftershave. "I'm Robert, by the way."

"It's nice to meet you, Robert. I'm Hannah." The fake name rolls off my tongue without hesitation.

It's much cooler when we step outside, and goosebumps race across my bare arms. The breeze carries a jazz melody through the air.

"First time at Raven's Hollow?" Robert asks, matching my pace on the winding path lined by evergreen trees.

"Yes."

"What brought you here?"

"Privacy," I answer.

"Should I take that as my cue to leave?"

I laugh. "No, I didn't mean that. I'm here to work, but I plan to take breaks and get the most out of the resort."

Another couple approaches us on the path. They've dressed up for the evening, she in a simple black cocktail dress and heels, and he in a tailored sports coat. We step aside, and Robert's hand hovers near my elbow, not quite touching.

"What sort of work do you do?" he asks once they've passed.

"I'm a writer."

"Ah, I'll bet this is a great place to write. The scenery and the isolation."

"Yes, exactly. What about you? What do you do, and what brought you here?"

"I needed a change of scenery, to get away, and time to think. Although my work has a way of following me. What do you write?"

He didn't tell me his profession, but I answer his question, anyway. "I write fiction books," I say, not wanting to go into the details.

Robert laughs at my curt response. "Anything I might have read?"

"Probably not."

That's a lie. My latest novel in the Darkness series has been on the bestseller lists and front display tables of every major bookstore for months.

"What's your last name, Hannah?"

"Williams." Only when I drop a fake surname am I uncomfortable about lying, but it's not a big deal. We're only going to have a drink together. After that, I'll probably never see him again.

The Summit Bar stands before us, all rough-hewn timber and glass. We push through doors thick enough for a fortress and claim two seats at the polished mahogany bar. In one corner, a duo plays a saxophone and piano, the music we heard earlier.

The lighting is intentionally low, but behind the bar, a showcase of premium liquors is well-lit by hidden fixtures around the glass shelves.

I pick up a menu that lists the bar's specialty cocktails in calligraphy. I love the names: Moonlit Maven, Alpine Reverie, Winter's Bliss. The Raven's Elixir looks the best. It's a mix of rum, blackberry liqueur, absinthe, bitters, and black currant syrup.

A bartender with a trim beard, plaid shirt, and black vest takes our order. He crafts our cocktails right in front of us, shaking mine before pouring it over crushed ice and placing a plump blackberry on the rim.

Robert's glass meets mine with a delicate clink. "To getting everything we want out of our vacation at Raven's Hollow."

"I'll drink to that." His toast makes me think about what I want—to finish my first draft. If the rest of the story flows as easily as it did today, I have a good chance of succeeding.

The way Robert watches me and moistens his lips makes my heartbeat quicken. I wonder what he wants.

I take a sip of my cocktail. The sharp taste of licorice follows the sweetness, making it unique and delicious.

Our conversation flows effortlessly, with no awkward pauses and nothing that makes me want to leave. I find myself leaning closer, drawn to his presence, and ordering another round of drinks. My skin is warm, and whenever I meet his gaze, it sparks an urge deep within me. I can't deny there is chemistry between us, enhanced by our drinks, no doubt. I'm usually cautious with my alcohol because I never want to lose control, but tonight, I'm okay with letting go. Not completely. I'm well aware of what I'm doing, but my inhibitions are loosening.

Time flies before I realize it's late, and I've finished another drink. "This was nice. It's just what I needed after working all day, but I better get some sleep so I can be productive in the morning."

Robert rises from his chair. "How long are you staying at the resort, Hannah?"

Now that we've had such a nice time together, I wince when he says the name that isn't mine. "Ten days. And you?"

"Another week."

"I'm in Elk Lodge," I hear myself say as we head out of the bar, alcohol making me braver, or more foolish.

"Same."

Anticipation creates a tingling sensation within me.

The journey back to Elk Lodge is charged with a little excitement and a lot of uncertainty. It could be the Raven's Elixirs coursing through my veins or the way Robert's shoulder brushes against mine in the darkness. My thoughts leap ahead to the way this night could end. His room or mine. Is that what I want? He's charming but a complete unknown, though perhaps that's why this is so exciting.

As we approach my door, he points to one across the hall and two down. We stop walking, and the air crackles with the unspoken intentions rippling between us.

Before he can speak, before I can change my mind, I give a small wave that's absurdly casual considering the current tension. I turn to my door, and my hands tremble as I search my purse for my key card.

Inside my room, as I go through my night routine of washing away makeup and brushing my teeth, I try to convince myself I made the right choice. I can only wonder what might have happened if our evening hadn't ended when it did.

We parted ways tonight, but for the rest of my time here, we know where to find each other.

CHAPTER 5

I lie alone in the large bed with the cool, crisp sheets against my skin. Not surprisingly, my thoughts turn to Robert. Something clicked between us tonight. Or at least, I think it did.

Since he's here for a week, I hope to see him again, but I don't want to get ahead of myself. My eyes close, and that's about all I remember until I'm jolted awake, gasping for air as if I've just escaped from a suffocating dream.

It's midnight, and I only got one hour of sleep. I roll onto my side, then my back, to find a comfortable position. When that doesn't work, I make mental lists, as I'm prone to do. Before long, I'm back to plotting my novel.

I'm trying to form a description of Hannah's captor, but Robert's face keeps appearing. There's just something about the resort guest down the hall with the dark lashes and half-smile. Or maybe it's just that I haven't spent much time with an attractive man in a long while.

As I lie awake, I replay our conversation in my head, enjoying bits of it all over again. I think of questions I'd like to ask him and conversations we might have in the future.

The thin mountain air can cause insomnia, and I think that's what's going on with me now. I've experienced it before and hoped to avoid the effects, but no such luck. With a defeated sigh, I cast off the covers. There's a wall switch by my bed, and I flick it now, flooding the room with light so I can head over to the desk. If I can't sleep, I might as well work.

By the time my laptop hums to life, I'm ready. Back to Hannah, my poor, innocent protagonist. Or is she? Everyone has secrets festering just beneath the surface. Perhaps she'll surprise readers and turn out differently from what they expect. Dangerous, even.

FROM THE MANUSCRIPT

Jarring movements.

Rattling noises.

Hannah emerged from a murky consciousness. Her arms ached, and grit pressed into her cheek. When full awareness hit, her heart slammed against her ribs. She forced her eyes open and found herself in a windowless utility van. The metal walls amplified every rattle and bang as they bounced over what felt like an endless dirt road. She tried to push herself up, but zip ties cut into her wrists and ankles.

She choked back a sob, terrified of drawing attention, of making whatever was happening even more terrible. Jackson must have seen something. Must have called someone, yet the absence of police sirens told her no one was coming yet.

She moved her bound hands over her coat pockets, searching for her phone. The memory hit her like a blow. She'd left it charging in the Tesla.

If she'd been conscious during the abduction, she could have mapped their route, counted the turns, listened for highway sounds or train tracks. Instead, she had no idea how long she'd been unconscious or how far they'd traveled. Now that she was awake, she started counting soundlessly. One, two, three...

The slow jolting journey continued, each teeth-rattling bump taking her further from safety, making no stops or turns. Hannah's terror grew, but she kept counting. One thousand one hundred forty-three. One thousand one hundred forty-four...

The vehicle finally lurched to a halt. Hannah tried to calculate how much time had passed since she'd started counting, but with fear addling her brain, she struggled to do the simple math.

One thousand six hundred and forty seconds equated to around twenty-six minutes. At the crawling pace they'd maintained—about ten miles per hour over the rough terrain, she was at least five miles from the nearest paved road.

The engine shut off. In the sudden quiet, her ragged breathing seemed too loud. Her fingers scrabbled around in search of a weapon, a screwdriver, or a piece of metal or glass. The floor was bare, and she came up with nothing.

"It's going to be okay," she told herself. "I'll do what he says. I'll survive this."

A door in the vehicle's front creaked open. Someone got out. The door slammed shut.

Hannah's heart pounded. She couldn't think or move.

The handle near her clicked, and the door slid open.

With some reluctance, I save my progress and close the manuscript. The writing session went well, but it's almost 4 a.m. My eyes are burning. I need to sleep.

As I climb back into bed and arrange the pillows, I force Hannah and her predicament out of my thoughts. I don't want my dreams to turn into nightmares.

CHAPTER 6

Purple shadows darken my eyes, and my skin has a waxy tone. Pressure squeezes my head, as if my brain didn't get enough time to detoxify itself or whatever it does while I sleep. I don't look my best. That's the price of working into the early morning hours, though the progress on my novel was worth it.

I'm not one for yoga, but my editor raved about the classes and suggested they would "open my creativity." Since I'm here for inspiration, I might as well try a class. The resort's website touts it as an exercise for the body and the soul. A class might balance out my lack of rest.

The sun shines over the mountain peaks as I follow a path to the yoga studio. At a fork, I find a charming directional sign with arrows pointing to various buildings. In my next book, perhaps my character will stumble across a similar sign, one with sinister destinations.

The fitness building is near the spa. Inside the studio entrance, I slip off my shoes, lining them up in a cubby with other pairs of athletic shoes and sandals. The only sounds come from light, ethereal music, and the tinkle of a water fountain. Floor-to-ceiling windows in the yoga studio frame yet another gorgeous mountain view.

After choosing a spot in the back corner, I select a mat, unfurl it, and settle into a cross-legged position. A couple nearby speak in soft voices as they fold forward, touching their toes. More guests enter and roll out their mats.

A cute, curvy woman with long brown hair chooses the open space next to me and unfurls her yoga mat.

"Can you believe the views?" she asks, her gaze on the mountains as she pulls her hair into a no-nonsense ponytail. "I can't imagine a more beautiful spot to practice yoga, can you?"

"No, I guess I can't."

She smiles at me. "Are you having a good stay here at the resort?"

"Yes. Impossible not to, right? Where are you from?"

"Charlotte," she answers.

"Oh. So am I."

Our conversation ends as the instructor moves to the front. She's a petite woman with dreadlocks.

"Good morning, everyone. I'm Letizia. Welcome to Raven's Hollow. I hope you're enjoying your time here. I'm grateful you've joined me for this class. Please move at your own pace and honor your body as we practice together." Her tranquil gaze surveys the room. "Let's begin by finding our center. Close your eyes and take a deep breath. Let go of the thoughts pulling you in different directions. Let your mind and body be still."

I try to follow her guidance, but I'm stuck thinking about the term *deep breath* and the number of times I've had to search my draft manuscripts for instances of the word *breath* and eliminate them because I've overused the word.

We continue with the breathing, holding and releasing our inhalations, as Letizia urges us to connect with our inner selves. The exercise goes on too long for my liking. I open my eyes and peek at the people around me.

Everyone else is following the rules. Good for them. I respect that; I do. Provided the rules are reasonable.

I stare out the window where the forest pines blend into an impenetrable wall of deep green with pointed tops around the resort. Finally, the asanas begin, and I flow through the poses, glad to be moving. Sitting for so long does a number on my back and neck, and these stretches help.

Letizia offers encouragement through challenging poses. "Stay with it, everyone. Breathe through the pose."

There's that word again—*breathe.* I think she overuses it more than I do.

I'm not having any trouble with the poses. I think I'm quite good at yoga, though the instructor already made a point of not comparing ourselves to others in the studio.

When the class concludes, and I'm rolling up my mat, the woman next to me starts up another conversation. "You have a beautiful practice. I can tell you're really into yoga."

"No, I'm not. This is a new thing for me, but thanks."

Something flickers across her face, as if she doesn't believe me, but then her smile is back. "I'm Sarah. And you are?"

"Hannah."

Sarah's smile wavers. "Hannah. Right. Well, it's nice to meet you." She hesitates like she wants to say more. "I hope I run into you again while we're both here. I'm traveling alone too, so if you ever want company, I'm in the Elk Lodge. Room 232."

I blink in surprise. Why does she think I'm at the resort alone?

We're interrupted when the instructor approaches us. "I hope you both got what you needed from the session. We're delighted to have you here at Raven's Hollow. Your presence is a gift to all of us."

I return her smile, trying not to laugh. Calling our presence a 'gift to all' is a bit excessive, but I'm glad I came. I feel energized and eager to get back to work.

CHAPTER 7

A fter yoga, I order brunch from room service, change into my comfy pink sweats, and sit at my desk to write. My characters are waiting. No one there can make a move without me.

FROM THE MANUSCRIPT

Hannah braced herself as the van's door screeched open. The interior light came on, revealing endless darkness and trees thrashing in the wind.

Her pulse pounded in her ears as her abductor stepped out of the shadows and into the light's glow. He didn't come across as evil or monstrous, as she expected, but more like someone she'd encounter at a sporting goods store. He was ruggedly handsome, with a firm jaw and a neatly trimmed beard. In a heavy brown coat, he looked solid and powerful, about ten years older than her, somewhere in his late thirties.

A violent shiver seized her body—not just from the freezing air rushing into the van, but from the crushing realization that he hadn't bothered to hide his face with a mask or blindfold her. She understood what that meant. His face might be the last she ever saw. She might not leave this place alive.

The man withdrew something from his coat pocket and flipped it open, exposing a sharp pocketknife.

Hannah winced, and her eyes instinctively closed, expecting the blade to slice through her skin. Instead, she heard a snap, and the bindings around her ankles fell away.

"Get out," the man commanded in a deep voice. He tugged her out of the van and onto the dirt road, her legs nearly buckling beneath her.

"What am I doing here?" she asked.

"You'll find out soon enough. And you don't have to be quiet. Go ahead, scream all you want. No one will hear you." His tone terrified her.

A massive shape hurtled toward them, then halted a few feet away, barking at Hannah.

"Down, Bolton."

At its master's command, the dog fell silent but kept its gaze trained on her.

Every cell in her body screamed to run, but she was terrified it might only worsen her situation. Cooperation might offer the best chance of survival.

Her vision adjusted, revealing the shadow of a pickup truck and a nearby building as the man grabbed her arm and steered her toward them.

She grasped at a strategy she remembered from abduction movies and books—make yourself human and relatable. Personal details can evoke empathy.

"I'm Hannah," she said in a quivering voice. "I live in Charlotte. Please, I don't understand why you took me."

His response was a cruel sneer as he dug his fingers deep into her arm and propelled her forward.

Bolton trailed behind them, emitting a low growl.

As they neared the building, motion-activated lights illuminated a log cabin with dark timber logs, a pitched roof, and a stone chimney. In different circumstances, Hannah would have thought it charming. It resembled the cabin she'd rented for her weekend with Jackson, except for one major difference. Her vacation cabin was clustered among others, not alone like this, miles from civilization and hidden in the wilderness.

"Why am I here?" Hannah asked again. She tried to sound reasonable and professional, as if this were a business meeting gone off schedule rather than an abduction.

The man wheeled around at the cabin's entrance, his face inches from hers. "You're not very good at listening, are you, Hannah? I said you'll find out when you need to."

Her gaze darted back to the van. Had he pocketed the keys or left them in the ignition? The detail might matter if she were to escape, but in her terror, she hadn't noticed.

"Please, let me go," she whispered. "I won't tell anyone, I swear. You can trust me."

He opened the cabin door. Bolton trotted in first, and she followed.

Recessed lights gleamed off wood-paneled walls in an open room containing the kitchen and living area. The entire space was clean and devoid of clutter. Mounted game trophies hung from most vertical surfaces. A stag's antlers spread like gnarled branches beside the head of a gray wolf, and the eyes of a red fox seemed to stare right into hers.

Hannah processed everything she saw. Orderly cabin. Hunting trophies. Her captor's demanding demeanor. All were signs of a person who thrived on power and control.

A landline phone hung beside the refrigerator on the opposite side of the room. If only she could use it.

Hannah cringed when the man unzipped her coat, slid it off her shoulders, and hung it in a closet by the front door.

"Sit," he said, pointing to a wooden chair.

Hannah hesitated, then did as she was told.

He removed a ceramic jug from a fridge packed with similar containers and poured an opaque liquid into a beer mug. As he raised the mug to his mouth, he stared at her in a way that made her skin crawl.

She forced herself to speak. "I have people who love me. My parents will do anything to get me back. Can I call them? Please."

He said nothing.

"Is it about money?" she asked. "They'll pay you." Her father would empty any accounts he had to help her. She was sure of that.

The man's eyes narrowed, and for an instant, Hannah thought he might say yes. Instead, his glare bore into her until she turned away.

Stay alive, she told herself. Just stay alive until they find you. Jackson must have law enforcement searching for her by now, and her parents would do anything to ensure her safe return. She had to wait it out. She prayed it wouldn't be too long before help arrived.

"Can I just use your phone? So I can tell my family I'm okay," she said, though she wasn't okay. Nothing about this situation was remotely okay.

"This isn't a sleepover at your friend's house. Now get up. Open that door. Move."

Hannah walked in front of him, through a door and down a narrow set of stairs made of unfinished wood. From there, he marched her into a small room with a bare bulb dangling from the ceiling. The space was barely larger than the college dorm room she'd complained about throughout her junior year because of its size.

The basement room contained a military-style cot and a metal table. An interior door led to a small bathroom with a toilet and shower. Neither room had windows.

The man took out his pocketknife again and freed her hands. "Sleep tight," he said in a menacing voice. "You'll need your strength for later."

"What happens later?" Her question escaped before she could stop it.

The door slammed. The bolt turned and clicked. His footsteps headed upstairs.

When she could no longer hear him, Hannah tried the door handle. She was locked in.

As she paced the confines of the windowless room, a claustrophobic panic took over her thoughts. She focused on the rise and fall of her chest to prevent hyperventilating. To survive this, she couldn't crack in the first hour.

Something on the wall sent a fresh wave of horror through her—tally marks scratched into the cement. Four vertical lines crossed by a fifth, repeated over and over and over. Someone else had been trapped in the room before.

She spun around and gasped at identical marks on another wall. She wasn't this man's first victim, nor his second. She was at least his third.

Hannah counted the second set of tally marks, then counted again, praying she'd made a mistake. One hundred and sixty days. Over five months.

She sank onto the cot in a feverish daze. What had the other captives endured? What happened when the scratch marks ended? Her captor had said she'd need her strength for later. What would happen then?

She lay down and pulled the thin blanket around her shoulders, though it did nothing to stop her shivering. She kept her eyes fixed on the door, afraid to fall asleep as exhaustion pulled at her. Her eyes grew heavy, and she struggled to keep them open, fighting to stay awake.

That's where I stop writing. Hannah isn't the only one falling asleep. I wrote that last part because the same thing is happening to me. I rarely nap, but I need one today because I got so little sleep last night.

As I get up from my desk and pad across the floor to the bathroom, I think about this character I've created. Hannah is a "good" person, and her fear is relatable, but her weakness bothers me. She might be dragging my whole story down. Readers might respect her more if she resisted and died fighting back. It's something to consider.

CHAPTER 8

After taking a quick nap and a long shower—fifteen minutes of excellent water pressure against my scalp and shoulders—I ditch my comfortable writing sweats for more presentable clothes. When I step into the corridor in my hip-hugging black dress, Robert's door opens. Our eyes meet, and we laugh because what are the chances of this happening unless one of us was waiting, ear pressed to the door, listening for signs the other was about to leave? I know I wasn't.

"Are you headed to dinner?" he asks.

"Yes, I'm famished, practically starving." The words tumble out before I notice my abandoned brunch tray is still outside my door. Half-finished plates with bacon quiche and steak salad do little to back up my claims of starvation. For someone who spends hours crafting sentences and carefully choosing words, I can fumble spectacularly in real conversations.

"Care for some company?" he asks.

"Sure. I'm headed to Raven's Watch Tavern." There's a cautious note in my voice, but it's only dinner. What harm could come from one meal?

Our excellent timing allows us a fireside table, and our conversation flows even easier than last night. I learn he's an IT consultant, but for now, he's keeping his private life to himself as much as I am.

"I was in Venice two summers ago. Have you ever been?" I ask before taking a sip of my wine.

"I haven't, but I once boarded a flight to Rome that ended up having mechanical issues. We had to get off the plane, and the flight scheduled for the next day got delayed over and over, then canceled as well. It was such an ordeal that I gave up on Italy and hopped on the next flight to Florida instead. So, I never made it to Italy, but somehow my suitcase did. Italy is still on my list."

"Wow, flying can be such a joy, huh?" I say with a laugh. "I hope you make it to Italy someday. It's amazing." I point toward the mountains outside. "Though if you love places like Raven's Hollow, I recommend Jackson's Hole."

"Yes," he says, his face lighting up. "I've been there three times. Love the place. Where did you stay?"

Our travel stories eventually run out, but we transition to movies and TV shows, keeping the lively conversation going throughout our meal. We both love binge-watching Netflix thriller series and devouring seasons of our favorite shows. With each topic we explore, my comfort level with Robert deepens. It's not because of any uncanny similarities, but simply the natural give and take between us. Our dinner is flying by.

"I had a massage yesterday," Robert says. "It was so great I booked another before leaving the spa."

I picture his bare shoulders under a masseuse's hands. "Maybe I should treat myself to one while I'm here. I heard they book up fast."

"If they're full, you can have my session. I'll feel guilty otherwise."

"That's very kind of you. Thank you," I say, appreciating his offer, though I'd feel more guilty about taking his session away from him.

As we discuss tomorrow's plans—his resort activities, my writing schedule—my mind drifts to Hannah. She's still locked in her fictional basement, unaware of the horrors that await. Those aren't pleasant dinner thoughts, but until I finish my novel, her story will always be with me, grabbing my attention when I least expect it and pulsing away in the back of my mind like an extra heartbeat.

"How was your meal?" the hostess asks when we're leaving.

"Mine was excellent. Please give my compliments to the chef on the venison," Robert says.

"I'm happy to do that for you. Are you in the mood to toast marshmallows? We have everything you need for s'mores."

Robert and I haven't discussed extending the evening, but I want to. "Why not?" I say, aiming for casual. "If you're up for it."

Robert accepts the marshmallow supplies with a boyish grin that makes my stomach flip, and we head to the firepit nearest Elk Lodge. The crisp evening has given way to a chilly night, increasing the appeal of cuddling around a fire with him.

When we reach the gas firepit, I notice Robert checking his watch, but I don't give it much thought. I unpackage our s'more supplies and begin skewering marshmallows.

Robert's technique is impeccable. His marshmallows are browning evenly, unlike mine.

"Haven't done this since my Boy Scout days," he says.

"You were a Boy Scout?"

"An Eagle Scout." A grin spreads across his face. "There's an art to this."

I lean closer, drawn in by his playful tone.

"There's a secret ingredient that makes them taste better."

"Oh? What would that be?" The words comes out breathier than I intended.

"The company of an accomplished and beautiful woman."

I roll my eyes because that was corny, but his words make my pulse jump. He's an intelligent and interesting guy, and I'm now enjoying every minute with him.

We assemble our s'mores, smashing the melted marshmallows between the graham crackers. As I lick the sticky sugar off my fingers, I'm hyper-aware he's watching me.

We laugh as we eat our sweet creations. His dessert leaves a smudge of chocolate on the corner of his mouth, and without thinking, I brush it away. When our eyes meet, he leans down and touches his lips to mine to deliver a soft and thrilling kiss.

I'm aware of voices growing louder, coming closer, and I reluctantly separate from Robert. A family arrives with their s'mores packets, and our romantic moment ends. Robert checks his watch again, and I hope it's not because there's some place else he'd rather be.

"I'm sorry. I have a meeting tonight," he says.

"Tonight?" We've just kissed, and now he's pulling away? "It's nine o'clock."

"One PM in Tokyo. I have to lead a call. That's why I went with marshmallows instead of drinks."

"Yes, it's the safer option if you have to be responsible and work," I say with a chuckle, though I'm disappointed.

"I want to see you tomorrow." His eyes hold mine, serious now.

"I'll check my schedule," I answer, teasing him.

There's another kiss just outside my door before we part. It's deeper, longer, and makes my head spin.

Alone in my room, I still feel Robert's lips on mine. I'm here to write a dark thriller about a woman's captivity and demise because that's what I do. But for the first time, I understand why authors write romance books and why people love to read them.

CHAPTER 9

V oices in the corridor interrupt my sleep.

A man's voice. "Hold on. I forgot my sunglasses. Wait for me."

A woman's response, "You're always forgetting something. Hurry."

They sound anxious to start the day, which compels me to do the same.

Once I'm out of bed, I'm pleasantly surprised to find the paper someone slid under my door isn't a bill estimate but a handwritten note.

Sorry I had to duck out last night. Does dinner at 7 work for you?

Robert's name isn't on the note, but it's from him. Who else could it be? Smiling inside, I grab a pen and, without debating over the perfect words the way I do with my novels, I jot down my answer.

See you at seven. Have a fabulous day.

I exit my room clutching my response and slip it under Robert's door, wondering when he'll discover it. I imagine he got up early and headed to the gym or out for a run. Judging by his appearance, he's disciplined with sports and workouts.

After breakfast and coffee, I return to my suite, ready to dive into my writing.

Unfortunately, Robert and last night's kiss still monopolize my thoughts. Transitioning from this bright, unexpected part of my stay into the mood required to write my disturbing novel presents a challenge.

As I read over the last chapter of my manuscript, clouds sweep across the sun, and dark shadows cover my desk. It doesn't take too long before I'm with Hannah in the isolated basement room where the cold seeps through the concrete walls.

I finish my writing session a few hours later and notice a chip in my nail polish. A quick call to the spa, and I get lucky. They have an opening for a full manicure and pedicure.

I arrive early and peruse the selection of colors, choosing a bottle labeled *Flame Kissed Red*. It's appropriate for my plans with Robert.

Our dinner is at a smaller, less formal restaurant called the Ski Side Grill. Vintage wooden skis with leather bindings and weathered snowshoes decorate the walls. There's a stone fireplace against one wall, though not a showstopper like the massive hearth inside Raven's Watch Tavern.

The restaurant is quiet until a large party arrives at the same time as our food. The fifteen or more of them transform the ambiance with their boisterous laughter and loud voices.

"I bet they're here for a wedding," Robert says.

Before I can stop myself, I ask, "Have you ever been married?"

I expect a simple "no." Instead, Robert answers, "Yes."

My hand flies to my chest. The night we met, I noticed he wasn't wearing a wedding band, but not all married men do. Some remove their rings to suit their needs. I should have asked sooner. The pitch of my voice rises as I ask, "Are you divorced?"

When he shakes his head, a wave of sickness washes over me. I glare at him. "Then what are you doing here?"

"My wife died." His eyes hold a deep sadness I hadn't noticed before.

"I'm so sorry." Of course, I feel terrible for him and her, but I'm also relieved I'm not on a date with a married man. "She must have been very young."

"Thirty-three."

Robert can't be much older than thirty-five, if he's even that old. If he and his wife were the same age, she had passed away recently. I'm already devising scenarios. Cancer. Car accident. Overdose. Suicide. Anorexia. I have no shortage of ideas.

"What happened?" I ask, prodding, but in a gentle tone. If I don't find out, I'll be thinking about it all night like an itch I can't scratch.

Robert responds, but the wedding party people erupt in laughter, and I don't hear the answer.

I lean forward across the table. "Sorry, I missed that. How did she die?"

"Rock climbing accident," he says, pressing a fist to his lips. "She fell. It was horrible,"

A gasp rises inside me. I hadn't considered something so, dare I say, interesting. As a psychological thriller writer, I've killed characters in so many ways, but never like that. "I'm truly sorry, Robert," I say. "I can't imagine."

"It was a shocker, even though we all understood the dangers. She was good, climbed all the time. Her death destroyed me for a while." Robert sniffs. "Turns out we never know how much time we have."

After that, I nurse my wine, giving him space to collect himself. Our cozy dinner has taken a turn into somber territory, and I steered us there. Still, I'm glad to have this information about Robert. His background and experiences are key to understanding his perspective. The sudden loss of a spouse must be devastating, and I expect she'll always own a piece of his heart. He's probably thinking about her now. I am, and I can't stop, thanks to the dark side of my creative brain. I'm suddenly obsessed with the specifics of her untimely death, particularly: Was Robert with her when she fell?

CHAPTER 10

Despite my earlier mood-dampening question, dinner turns into drinks again. Tonight, we forgo the bar stools and sit together on a leather bench alongside a wall of windows.

Holding our cocktails, we keep moving closer to each other. I'm not sure if it's simply natural chemistry or the influence of my Raven's Elixir and his second scotch on the rocks. It's as if I've known him for much longer than two days.

Robert props his chin on his hand, his eyes holding mine with an intensity that makes my skin tingle. "Don't be upset about this," he says, "but it's important to me to learn a little about the people I'm with. I Googled you last night."

A knot forms and twists in my stomach. I'd forgotten that I've been lying about my name, and he thinks it's Hannah Williams. He's searched for someone who doesn't exist. This isn't good.

"There are a lot of Hannah Williams out there," he says. "I found some authors, but none who write thrillers. None of them were you."

"Like I said, few people have heard of me." The lie makes me wince inside.

"You can do things to change that. There are lots of options. Get a website and some social media presence. You could run some paid ads on Facebook or Instagram. I could help."

"Thanks, but that's not my thing."

He nods with a skeptical expression but lets the topic drop. I'm okay with letting him think I'm an author no one has ever heard of. I prefer my privacy, and I don't know him all that well, although that's changing quickly.

As the night progresses, brushes against each other's arms and legs evolve into deliberate touches. There's the heat of his hand on my thigh, the subtle pressure of his fingers through the fabric of my dress. His presence ignites a spark inside me, a thrilling warmth, and conversations from the bar's other patrons fade into the background.

Before I realize it, we're leaving the bar, arms linked. I want to be cautious, but the passion between us is overwhelming my reservations.

At my door, I fumble with the keycard, and it nearly slips from my grasp. My hands are shaky with a dizzying mix of anticipation and nerves. A sexual encounter with a hot stranger is the last thing I expected when I booked my writing retreat.

The door swings open, and as it clicks shut behind us, any lingering hesitations vanish.

Our hands are all over each other, my flushed skin tingling at his touch.

As Robert's lips leave mine, tracing a path down my neck, he murmurs, "Hannah."

For a fleeting second, I question if I will regret this.

Much later, Robert slips from beneath the sheets and heads to the bathroom. While he's in there, I turn on the bedside lamp, grab a sleep shirt from my dresser, and pull it over my head.

When he returns, he's wearing only boxers, and his body is all lean muscle and the ideal angles. He works out. As he pauses by my books on the shelf about my dresser, my admiration turns to unease.

"I've heard of Zipporah Bazile," he says. "Am I saying that right?"

"Perfect pronunciation," I answer, my heart thumping faster.

He lifts *Her Darkest Lies* from the shelf, studies the cover, and flips it over. The book contains no author photos to reveal my identity. I could continue with the charade of being Hannah Williams, but if our relationship has any chance of becoming more than a vacation fling, the lies have to end.

I swallow, pull on my ear, and say, "Those books are mine."

"You brought them with you to read? That's a lot of reading for the time you're here if you're also writing, isn't it?"

"No. That's not what I mean." I sit on the edge of the bed, still debating if I should tell the truth. And then I do. "They're mine because I wrote them. I'm Zipporah Bazile."

He turns to me. "I don't understand. Is this your pen name?"

"No. It's my real name. The name I was born with. My friends and family call me Zip."

"Oh." He strokes his chin, eyes fixed on the shelf. His profile gives nothing away. I can't tell if he's angry or confused. "So, who is Hannah Williams?"

"The name I used to check in for the sake of my privacy. I hope you can understand why I didn't tell you. Who could have imagined this would happen between us?"

"That explains why I couldn't find anything about an author named Hannah Williams online." He lets out a soft laugh. "I felt a little sorry for you, a struggling author with no online presence." He studies the book in his hands. "You're a *big* deal, aren't you?"

I draw my knees to my chest. My lie has weakened our connection. "I'm sorry I didn't tell you sooner."

Robert puts *Her Darkest Lies* back on the shelf. "It's okay. I get it."

"What about you?" I tuck a strand of hair behind my ear, eager to move the focus away from myself. "I'd like to hear more about your work."

"Sure." He returns to the bed and slides in next to me. "No big surprises. I really am an IT consultant."

"When I hear IT consultant, I picture the Geek Squad. You've heard of them, right? I'm in awe of anyone who can fix computers and do all the technical stuff. I can fix plot holes, but when my computer breaks, my only hope is rebooting."

"Geek Squad, huh?" His eyes sparkle with amusement, and he strokes his fingers along my arm as he speaks. "Not officially, but I am a geek, and I also have a team. I guess you could call them a squad. I specialize in cybersecurity penetration testing."

"That sounds fascinating and dangerous, but your job, what you do, is still a mystery to me."

He smiles. "My team gets hired by large corporations to find the weaknesses in their systems. We're red teamers. Good guys pretending to be bad guys."

"Oh, you're a professional hacker?"

"With permission," he adds.

"How long have you been doing that?"

"Thirteen years. I started my company after college with two friends. Now we've got over a hundred specialists." There's pride in his voice, but it's his humility that impresses me. He didn't offer the information until I prodded, which speaks volumes about his character.

Robert seems to have forgiven me for giving him a false name, and things between us are comfortable again, but I have a nagging thought as we lie beside each other. We've had two nights of endless conversation, and only now are we discovering who we really are. What other truths haven't we told each other?

CHAPTER 11

I'm not alone in the morning. Robert sleeps soundly beside me, his body radiating heat. I observe him, noticing the slight stubble on his face that wasn't there before and how different he looks with his hair falling over his forehead. Last night, I drifted off to sleep with my head against his arm while he was telling me stories about his work. Not that I wasn't interested, but it was late. I was tired, and although I had some doubts, I felt safe lying next to him.

With the effects of alcohol and endorphins out of my system, I'm not as comfortable. I'm self-conscious and a little wary about him spending the night in my room. My knowledge of him is minuscule compared to what I don't know.

To ease my concerns, I search for ways to reassure myself he's a good man. A safe man. The success of his company suggests stability, and steadiness equals safety, though not always. Certainly not with the character I've created for Hannah's captor. He's dangerous but also calm and composed. Serial killers are often the most mild-mannered individuals, hiding behind charming behavior, and Robert is intelligent and exudes charm.

I slide toward my side of the bed, putting distance between us. Rather than reassuring myself that everything is going to be okay, I'm further convinced I have reasons to worry.

Robert stirs awake, stretching his arms as he opens his eyes. "Good morning, *Zip,*" he says, emphasizing my name.

"Good morning."

"Is this weird for you?" He props himself on his side, his elbow on the pillow.

"I don't usually do this sort of thing."

"I'm glad to hear that. Same here. It's been a long time." He presses his lips to my forehead before getting up, collecting his scattered clothes, and going into the bathroom.

In his absence, I wonder if I'm his first since his wife. If so, he showed little hesitation.

When he returns, dressed in last night's clothes, he heads straight to my bookshelf. "What's your current book about? Is it set at an isolated mountain resort?"

"Maybe." I offer a cryptic smile.

"Attractive, bestselling thriller author meets a geeky IT executive at Raven's Hollow Lodge and ... " He extends his hand for me to finish the sentence, but I don't because I want to hear his version. Instead, he shrugs. "Obviously, I'm not a writer."

"Thank goodness. There are already more books in the world than anyone could read in a few lifetimes. Cybersecurity seems more essential. And there's nothing geeky about you, at least not the way you look."

His laugh fills the room. "What are you calling your new book? The one you're working on?"

"Untitled."

"That's the title?"

"For now. Until I come up with one that's a perfect fit for the novel."

He stretches again, fingers laced above his head. "I'm going to leave and head back to my room. Do you drink coffee in the morning?"

"Coffee is non-negotiable. And breakfast. Seems I worked up an appetite." I grin, and he seems to appreciate my humor.

"Meet you in fifteen?" he asks, on his way to the door.

"Um, make it thirty."

After he leaves, I shower and get dressed. My phone chimes as I'm putting on some makeup, and my mother's name lights up the screen.

"Anything exciting happen?" she asks. There's a mischievous tone in her question, almost as if she's aware I spent the night with a great guy. A guy I've just met. Not that I'm having any regrets, but a rush of heat creeps across my cheeks like a sudden fever.

"No," I tell her, omitting the unexpected highlight of my trip so far. "Just writing. I'm about to grab a coffee. The resort's beautiful. I can't forget to thank Donna for suggesting it."

"Well, you insisted on going somewhere special to write your book."

I laugh. "That's true. Hey, I was up late, and I need my caffeine fix. Can I call you back later?"

"Of course, dear. We're always here for you."

As I hang up, those last words are a reminder of the unconditional support that anchors me. I can't imagine if that faded away or suddenly disappeared, like Robert's wife—here one moment, gone the next.

The thought makes my skin prickle as I leave my room to see him again.

CHAPTER 12

S hortly after our planned time, Robert and I take seats at The Raven's Nest Café and order coffee and breakfast. Our small table has a view of the mountains covered with misty fog.

"So, Zipporah Bazile." Robert draws out my name as he speaks it. "I noticed there aren't any photos of you online."

We were only apart for thirty minutes, and he searched the Internet about me. I can't say I blame him, yet it's still disappointing.

"That's right, no photos, intentionally." I lean closer, lowering my voice so no one will overhear. "I'd appreciate it if you'd keep who I am between us."

He draws an imaginary zipper across his lips. "My lips are zipped."

I chuckle, giving him credit for the clever wordplay with my name.

"After reading about your work, which is impressive, I'd sure like to know how you managed to write so many novels."

"Ah, well, I've always wanted to write, so I do. Writing is part talent and part learned skill, but mostly it's stubborn persistence. The key is to write as often as possible for as long as possible. Keep my butt in my chair and my fingers on the keyboard. That's my goal. Getaways like this help my productivity a lot." My words flow because I've shared this answer in off-screen interviews so many times that it's practically muscle memory. It may sound rehearsed, but it's the truth.

"I hope I haven't derailed your productivity too much." Robert's grin carries a hint of last night's activities, and I can't help but blush.

"No, you're a welcome distraction. Have you seen The Shining? All work and no play."

His smile widens, reminding me just how handsome he is. "We can't have you haunting Raven's Hollow's corridors, and I appreciate you making time for me. I enjoy being with you, and I want to continue."

I love his candor, and I feel the same way, though it frightens me almost as much as it thrills me.

"Tell me about *Untitled*," he says.

"Okay. It's about a woman named Hannah."

"The woman you checked into the hotel as. Now I get it."

"Well, not exactly. She and I have nothing in common, thank goodness. It's a dark psychological thriller—" Movement catches my eye, and I stop talking. Sarah from the yoga class walks toward us in workout pants and a ballet-neck top.

"Hi, Hannah." Her gaze flicks to Robert and stays there like she's studying him. "You two enjoying breakfast?"

"Yes. It's great," he answers, smiling. "You know each other?"

Sarah nods as I say, "We met in yoga. Turns out we're both from Charlotte."

"Let me take a photo of you two," Sarah offers.

"Sure, thanks. Kind of you." Robert offers his phone before I can refuse the picture with a polite, "No, thank you." And now it's too late to object. I'll have no control over this photo since it will live on his phone.

Sarah waves her hand sideways. "You need to get closer if you're both going to be in it."

Robert scoots his chair toward mine.

"One, two, three," she says. "Wait. Smile, Hannah. Good, there you go. Perfect. A few more, just in case."

I force a smile, but Sarah's is genuine when she hands the phone back to Robert. "I'm sure I'll see you both around. Enjoy your day."

"She seems nice," Robert says as Sarah leaves the café.

"Hmm, yes." I hesitate, then continue, "Um, Robert, if you have any social media accounts, please don't post any pictures with me in them."

He nods, and I hope he's not offended. At least I didn't ask him to delete the image.

As Sarah passes by the window, my eyes fix on the spa across from the café. "I should book a massage before they fill up," I say. "I'm just going to run over there and do that now while we're waiting for our food."

"Go ahead. I'll be here."

Scheduling a massage appointment only takes a few minutes, but I needed those minutes to calm down. It's just a photo, I tell myself. It's not a big deal.

When I return to the café, I find the server delivered our food and drinks while I was gone. I smile when I see two perfect foam hearts floating atop my latte, but my excitement soon turns to confusion. There's a chunky white powder in the foam. My writer's brain spins with dark possibilities. Crushed pills. Poison. Despite my dire need for caffeine, I won't be drinking this.

I catch Robert watching me, eyes narrowed.

"Is something wrong?" he asks.

"I changed my mind about the coffee."

"But you didn't even taste it yet."

I shrug and tear a piece from my croissant, examining it before popping it into my mouth. Years of writing thrillers have taught me a few things: it's better to be safe than sorry, and paranoia can keep you alive.

CHAPTER 13

E ach bland sip of the coffee I made in my room reminds me of the artisanal latte I abandoned earlier. Did I see an unusual clumping of powder in the foam, or am I letting my imagination distort reality? I wish I'd taken a photo, so I'd have some proof. The evidence is gone now, just like my peace of mind. With a sigh, I force my attention back to Hannah's story, where I control everything.

FROM THE MANUSCRIPT

Hannah jerked awake on the narrow cot, her shoulders stiff, her fingers aching from the cold. How long had she been out? Without her phone, she had no way to tell. She got up to use the bathroom, and when she returned, a sliver of light came from under the door's edge. That light hadn't been there when her captor locked her in.

She crept forward on the concrete floor and gripped the door handle. To her shock, the door opened. She scanned the room beyond, saw no one, and continued moving to the stairs. Also deserted.

Hannah tiptoed her way up, alert for any sign of her captor.

Lights were on in the cabin, but outside the windows, it was still dark. Her eyes went to the landline phone on the wall, and she hurried over. Shaking, she pressed nine-one-one, then registered the silence against her ear. No dial tone.

A noise from the hallway made her whirl around, heart pounding. She waited, but the cabin stayed silent. This was her chance. She wanted to burst out of the cabin and escape, race down the road to safety, but she'd have to cover miles to get there. Without more clothes, she'd freeze. When she opened the closet door, it was empty. Her coat was gone, along with all the other clothes she'd seen hanging there when she arrived.

A large flannel shirt hung over the back of a chair. It wasn't much, but she snatched it up. Back at the door, she turned the deadbolt and then the lock on the doorknob, expecting to hear a shout, or an alarm announcing her escape. The locks released, and the door opened. It was easy. Too easy. Every instinct screamed she was walking into a trap.

The van and truck waited outside. Unless her captor had a third vehicle, he was somewhere nearby.

The motion-activated lights blazed as she fled from the porch. Afraid that any second a hand would grab her shoulder and yank her back, she made a mad dash toward the darkness and freedom. Twenty-six minutes by van. How long on foot? The searing cold pierced through her clothing and made her skin ache. Each inhale felt like a stab of ice in her lungs as she stumbled over invisible ruts in the road. She ran as if her life depended on it because she believed it did.

His voice boomed out of nowhere. "Better move faster! I have excellent aim."

Hannah gasped and kept running, eyes wide with terror, every muscle burning.

A gunshot exploded in the darkness, and its echo rolled after her like thunder.

With adrenaline flooding her body, she pushed harder, gulping for air, until her foot sunk into a ditch and her ankle twisted. A sharp pain shot through her leg as she pitched forward onto the gravel road.

Not far behind her, the man laughed as she scrambled up.

"You're one hell of a disappointment. I thought you'd be faster and in better shape. And sticking to the road is stupid."

Bolton's barking intensified her fear. Fresh pain shot through her ankle when she put weight on it. Gasping, she cast desperate glances toward the pitch-black woods on either side of the road. Could she get through? One wrong step could send her over a cliff. The dog would track her, anyway. Finally, she screamed. "Help! Help me!"

The man grabbed her and swung her around. Green night vision goggles gave his face an alien quality. "That was your practice run. Next time, I'll give you more of a head start. And if you want a chance, don't stick to the road."

Bile rose in Hannah's throat as he dragged her back to the cabin, each step agony in her ankle. He'd set the scene, letting her believe she had a chance of getting away. He wanted her to run.

After forcing her back into the basement room, he locked the door again.

Hannah collapsed on the bed, shivering uncontrollably. She tucked her frozen hands between her thighs. Her sobbing filled the empty room.

The door opened again within minutes. He'd brought a plate of food—meat and potatoes—but no apologies, no explanation for what had just happened.

"Why?" Hannah asked between sobs. "Why are you doing this?"

He set the food down in silence.

"Please. I'm not a runner. I do yoga, hardly any cardio." He didn't care about her or her exercise routine, but terror spilled words from her mouth.

"Eat this, then sleep tight." His voice carried no emotion. "You need strength to improve on tonight's pathetic performance."

"But I hurt my ankle," she cried as he shut the door.

Hannah knew he didn't care. A wave of despair crashed over her. She finally understood why she was here. He'd trapped her and made her an unwilling participant in his sadistic game.

I place my hands on my desk and push away from my computer. I write dark and disturbing scenes for a living. The most gruesome parts are merely implied. They exist off the pages, so I don't horrify my readers, but those scenes are quite real in my mind. Even when I don't share them in my novels, I see them playing out in my head. Yet, this one bothers me more than any other.

I don't like Hannah's weakness and helplessness, but for now, I leave the story alone.

CHAPTER 14

After writing that last grim chapter, I need fresh air. First, I email my manuscript to myself so I can print a hard copy from my phone. Surely, the main lodge has a business center with printers. I'll search for one after lunch.

I slip my feet into sandals and then step out of my suite, half hoping to run into Robert. Instead, I see Sarah coming down the corridor. She's dressed in black riding boots and tan britches.

"Missed you in yoga today," she says, her smile bright.

I could explain about working, but that might lead to questions about what sort of work I do, and I'd prefer not to lie. Instead, I ask the obvious, "Are you going for a ride?"

"Yes, I'm on my way there now," she says. "Would you like to come with me? I'll bet they have another horse for you."

"Oh, no. Thank you. I love to ride, but I have things to do today. I'll book a trail ride for later in the week. You have fun."

"You, too. Enjoy your day. I'm sure I'll see you around." Her tone carries an odd certainty as she walks away.

Outside, beneath my hat and sunglasses, I weave through families and couples in athletic attire to grab a sandwich, then make my way to the main lodge.

I enter through a side door and pass doors labeled as conference rooms, private dining areas, and the movie theater. When I get to the lobby, I spot a narrow room with computers and printers.

I open my manuscript on my phone, select print, then spot a sheet of paper atop the printer. I'm about to set it aside when the title grabs my attention.

Zipporah Bazile—Wikipedia

Zipporah Bazile is an American author famous for her series of Darkness novels featuring heroine Katya Strauss. Bazile writes in the mystery and suspense genres and has won numerous awards for her work, including...

I read the first few sentences, then look around. I'm alone, but someone left this here. Who would have printed this, and why? I tear the paper into pieces and discard it in a nearby waste bin.

My gut tells me Robert might be the culprit. After all, who else is aware of my presence here? The thing bothering me most is that I specifically told him I wanted to stay under the radar, yet he left my Wikipedia page lying on the printer. I shouldn't jump to conclusions. Maybe it wasn't him but another guest reading my *Darkness* series who wanted some basic information on me.

I knead the back of my neck as my manuscript prints, then gather the pages and head straight for the front desk.

The same cheerful woman who checked me in on my first day watches me approach.

"Excuse me," I say. "Do you have a clip I can use for these?" I hold up my manuscript so she understands what I mean.

While she rifles through a drawer, I ask, "Did you notice who was using the business center earlier?"

"Sorry, we don't track who uses the business room." She offers me a small silver clip, like the kind I use to close the tortilla chip bags at home. "Are you having problems with the equipment?"

"No. Not that. It's nothing."

"Is there anything else I can help with?"

"Yes. Horseback riding. How do I arrange a ride?"

"You can visit the stables or call them if you prefer. The number is on your resort map. Do you need another copy?"

"I've got one. Thank you."

As I turn from the desk, my thoughts go back to the paper I found on the printer. It's too easy for someone to dig into my life with a quick online search, and I don't like it.

I'm safe from the bother as long as I remain in my suite and write.

CHAPTER 15

A t the lodge entrance, I review a schedule of resort activities posted on an easel. One activity stands out: 1pm—Archery Clinic.

That gives me an idea.

I've never held a bow, but Hannah's abductor has. He's as proficient with a bow and arrow as he is with a gun. This is my opportunity to understand what it's like to take aim and target one's prey, and it will help make my writing more authentic.

I retrace my steps back to the registration desk. "Back again." I smile. "Just noticed there's an archery lesson today. Where is it located?"

"Participants meet at the equipment lodge. That's also on your resort map." She checks her watch. "The clinic starts in fifteen minutes."

That's not enough time to return to my suite and get ready, but I do it anyway because I can't practice archery while holding my manuscript, and I'm not comfortable setting it down anywhere outside my room.

Pumping my arms, I power-walk to Elk Lodge, prioritizing what I need to do. Once inside, I place my printed manuscript on my desk while I'm kicking my sandals off and almost fall over when I yank my shorts down. I change into a sports bra, comfortable T-shirt, shorts and socks, and athletic shoes.

I'm on the verge of flying out the door when I stop and spin around. My manuscript. It's on the desk, alone and exposed, the word *UNTITLED* in caps and underlined on the top page. Crossing the room in five quick strides, I gather the pages, almost cradling them in my arms. After a few seconds of indecision, I insert my story between two summer sweaters in the closet, pulling the top one forward to hide the pages. Confident that my story is safe, I leave and jog-walk across the resort to the equipment lodge.

A small group has already gathered around the instructor, listening to his explanations. Among the participants is Robert.

Robert hasn't seen me yet, which gives me a chance to observe him. I hang back in the shadows like one of my fictional stalker characters. Everything about Robert is still new to me, and I'm noticing things I hadn't before. Things I appreciate, like the way he gives the instructor his full attention, nodding at precise moments, unlike the man next to him fiddling on a phone, which I find rude. Despite my appreciation, I can't help wondering if he stopped in the business center today and printed the Wikipedia page I found.

Robert is accepting his bow and quiver from the instructor when he spots me. I wave, and he comes right over.

"Hey, this is a surprise. Nice to see you."

"Likewise," I say, and though I thought of him with suspicion just minutes ago, his smile changes that.

"Taking a break from writing?" he asks as we walk with the group to the archery range.

"Yes. I wrote a chapter this morning, then went to the business office, and that's when I saw the info about archery right before it started. I ran to my room to change."

I wait for Robert to mention he also used the business center today and maybe we just missed each other, but he doesn't. Instead, a young woman to his left—attractive with blonde highlights, flouncy curls, and a flat, bare midriff—accidentally pokes him in the shoulder with her bow.

"Oh, I'm so sorry. Are you okay?" She touches his arm in a way that makes me think the poke might not have been accidental or she's glad it happened.

"I'm good. No worries," Robert answers.

"I've never done this," she says, continuing the conversation. "How about you?"

"I've got some experience. Target practice only. It's a great way to de-stress when you need to."

"Oh. If you're an expert, I'll stick with you." She tosses her hair as she moves closer to him. "Maybe you can share some tips."

The exchange continues, the woman clearly enjoying Robert's attention. A twinge of insecurity strikes me as I watch them interact. I'm not the only one here who finds him attractive.

Their conversation ceases when the instructor demonstrates the proper way to hold the bow and nock an arrow, followed by the fundamentals of aiming and releasing. I try to absorb every detail, and I hope I'll also get some new ideas for my story.

Each of us has a bullseye target. I'm positioned on one side of Robert. The flirty blonde woman is on the other.

I mimic the motions the instructor showed us, but my first arrow misses the target and lands in the dirt. Another attempt yields the same result.

Robert already has two arrows in the red circle, as close to the yellow center as they can get without being inside it. Poised to shoot another, his stance is relaxed, as though he has done this a thousand times before, and there's strength in his stillness. He draws the bowstring back, then releases the arrow. It whizzes straight into the center of his target.

The woman beside him lets out a loud whoop that changes to a purr. "Someone was being modest earlier. You're so good. Maybe you can give me a private lesson later."

She's not even trying to disguise her intentions, and her directness makes me smile. There's nothing wrong with going after what you want. I admire that, though it's stirring up an odd mix of emotions inside me.

I drown out their banter and refocus on my target, drawing back the bowstring. When I release it, my arrow goes wide and hits the ground again.

My next arrow hits the outermost ring, and that's enough for me.

"Well done, Zip. You've got some talent," Robert says.

"That's debatable, but thank you." I'm secretly pleased he's paying attention to me, despite the distraction to his left.

As the clinic ends, Robert asks if we can get together tonight for dinner. The way he smiles at me, I'm certain it's the after-dinner part he's thinking about, and I must admit I am, too.

That small victory accompanies me back to my suite.

CHAPTER 16

I have a few hours left before dinner, and I aim to write one more chapter. While I was learning the basics of archery, Hannah remained stuck in her basement prison. After getting hunted like prey, she's cold, exhausted, hungry, and growing more despondent with every passing hour. Things are about to get worse for her.

FROM THE MANUSCRIPT

Hannah's swollen ankle pulsed with pain. She lay on her back and kept it elevated in the air, wishing she had an ice pack. A foul odor emanated from the meat on the plate beside her. She'd devoured the potatoes hours ago, but hunger still gnawed at her insides. Sleep had come in restless bursts, and she couldn't say how much time had passed.

She was supposed to be sitting in front of a crackling fire with Jackson, sipping spiked hot cocoa, tasting the assortment of crackers, cheeses, and dried fruit she'd packed, wearing the matching plaid slippers she'd bought them. Not this.

Her fingers worked mechanically at the paper towel that came with her meal, tearing it into smaller and smaller shreds again and again until it resembled confetti. When nothing remained to tear, she collected the tiny scraps from the floor into her palm, hobbled to the bathroom, and dropped them into the toilet. There was little else for her to do.

The bathroom contained a collection of hotel-sized soaps, shampoos, and lotions, and Hannah needed a shower. Grime covered her skin from her sweat and fear, but getting naked and becoming even more vulnerable in his space made her stomach turn. Instead, she used the soap under her arms, only removing one sleeve of her shirt at a time.

The door clicked. Every muscle in her body tensed as she swung her gaze around, dropping the soap and pulling her shirt into place. A crack of light shone through beneath the door again.

This time was different, his twisted intentions clearer. He wanted her to run. What would happen if she refused to play along? Remembering the fury in his eyes and the tally marks that abruptly stopped, she didn't dare find out.

Hannah put her shoes on, wincing as the material pressed into her ankle. She grabbed the blanket for extra protection, wrapped it around her shoulders, and limped out of the room.

Upstairs, the cabin appeared quiet and empty as snow fell in fat flakes outside the windows. She zeroed in on the wall-mounted phone and lifted the receiver again. Still no dial tone. Her eyes darted around. What could she use to improve her chances? She opened the fridge and grabbed the only items she recognized. A water bottle and an apple. Survival basics.

The coat closet remained empty. She ventured down a shadowy hallway, worried her captor might be lurking behind a closed door. The first door was locked, and the second a bedroom. Hannah raided the closet, yanking clothing off hangers and frantically putting them on, aware he might come upon her any second. She bundled herself in two flannel shirts and a heavy sweater, the blanket over them like a cloak. She desperately needed a flashlight to guide her through the woods, but she didn't have one.

The storm ambushed her when she opened the door. She halted on the porch. As soon as she stepped in the snow, her tracks would lead him straight to her.

The van and truck were in front, heaped with snow. Instead of taking the obvious direct route, she edged along the outer cabin wall, favoring her good ankle, keeping to the snow-free area beneath the thick trees.

She hobbled around to the far side of the truck, its bulk obscuring the cabin's view. Any second, she expected to hear his voice or his dog, but it was the creak of the cabin door she heard first.

"I can tell you're behind the truck," he said, the calm tone of his voice making it extra frightening. "I'm going back inside and giving you five minutes to escape. Go, Hannah!"

She was too terrified to move.

"Go!" he shouted.

As she turned to run, a ledge of snow cascaded from the truck's side, revealing a gold and green emblem on the vehicle's door. The emblem was unmistakable—the insignia of the North Carolina Sheriff's Department.

With a burst of hope, she screamed, "Help! I'm here! He kidnapped me! Help!"

Her captor's laughing response cut through her screams. "Who the hell are you yelling for? You think anyone can hear you?"

Her hope died as she realized the truck had been there for days. If the sheriff had come searching for her, where was he now? Was her captor bold enough to take down law enforcement and make the sheriff disappear? But surely the truck had a tracker inside. Help must be coming. Eventually, the police would come after the sheriff, but for now, Hannah only had herself. She lurched into the woods.

She'd only gone about ten yards when a branch snagged the blanket and pulled it off her shoulders. A few more steps and her water and apple tumbled from her frozen hands. Snow-laden branches scratched her face, drenched her shoes and jeans, and made her legs raw and numb.

Every push forward met resistance. Thick brambles tore at her clothes. Combined with downed trees and bushes, they made her trek impossible. When she finally stumbled back on the dirt road, the cabin still in sight, her hands had lost all sensation from the cold.

She made another attempt to enter the woods and had to turn around. Again and again, she plunged in, her desperation growing and the loud crunch of her boots giving her location away.

A flying object zinged past her ear. Hannah stared in shock at the black arrow piercing the tree where her head had been seconds ago. She hadn't heard him coming.

She searched for a hiding place, but the forest wouldn't let her through. Trembling, she collapsed beside a thick tree trunk with her hands covering her head until she heard him approach. "Please," she pleaded. "Please, just let me go. I won't tell anyone."

"You aren't even close to having a chance to tell anyone. You're pathetic. The worst."

He dug his fingers into her arm and dragged her back to her prison.

He left Hannah with the soaked clothes she'd taken from his closet, but her blanket was gone.

Someone will come for the sheriff, she told herself as she shivered. Someone will come.

In the bathroom mirror, her skin was red and mottled where tears had frozen on her cheeks. Cuts covered her face. A deep scratch extended from the side of one eye down to her chin. Her fingers tingled with pain as they thawed.

She was still shivering when the man returned, carrying a pair of socks and another meal. He threw the socks at her chest and plunked a plate of carrots and potatoes onto the table. Then he slid an object from the front pocket of his plaid shirt.

Hannah's eyes locked on the object in his hand—a tarnished gold badge with the word SHERIFF across the top.

He held the badge up to her face.

"What did you do to him?" Hannah whispered.

Her captor laughed, a cruel sound that resonated through the small room. "What did I do to him? You still don't get it, do you?" He loomed over her, making her feel small and helpless. "I *am* him, sweetheart. North Carolina's finest, at your service."

Hannah gasped.

"That's why no one's coming. I've made clear this area got thoroughly searched. I guaranteed it myself."

His words were like icy tendrils squeezing the life from her heart. The terrifying truth destroyed her entire understanding of safety and hope.

Help wasn't coming. No one was going to find her because a sheriff told everyone she wasn't there.

His evil voice lingered in her head long after he left, when her still aching hands reached for the socks he'd brought. They were rough and gray, once white, but thick. She pulled them on, hating herself for her gratitude. In a twisted way, as long as he kept her locked in here, she needed her captor. He was all she had.

How many more hunts would she endure before he tired of her?

I stop typing there. After writing Hannah into her darkest moment so far, I need a break.

Her helplessness still bothers me. I should push her to change because strong novels require that sort of character growth, but I can't do it. I'm compelled to continue with her steady collapse.

CHAPTER 17

As I walk the resort path leading away from Elk Lodge, I'm grateful I have my dinner with Robert later. I still suspect he's responsible for the Wikipedia printout and he's been researching me every chance he gets, but I'm trying not to let that bother me. Paranoia has plagued me since I arrived, and it's distracting. If I want my anxiety to subside, I have to stop feeding it with my attention.

Across from the main building, ravens with iridescent black feathers perch in the branches of a tall evergreen. I researched ravens for one of my *Darkness* novels. When they're together, it's called an unkindness of ravens for their habit of gathering around death. I prefer to call them a flock.

The ravens take flight, soaring and shrieking above me as I climb the stone stairs to the lobby. That's where I see Robert again.

He's sitting on a leather couch, his phone pressed to his ear, and he doesn't notice me come in.

Allowing him privacy to finish his call, I head to the main desk. I'm not deliberately eavesdropping, but the lobby is empty, and voices travel easily. His tone captivates me. He sounds confident, yet conspiratorial, like someone sharing a secret.

"That works," he says. "That will do the job."

And then I hear, "Zipporah Bazile." My name. I could have been mistaken. I might have heard something similar to my name, but I doubt that. Not much sounds similar to Zipporah Bazile.

Robert's next words turn the blood in my veins to ice. "She can't find out. Not until it happens."

My mouth is open in shock as Robert turns in my direction.

"I have to go," he says into his phone. "Zip, hey." He's up and walking toward me. "Didn't expect to see you. I thought you were writing."

"Who were you talking to?"

"Just work stuff," he says with all the confidence of an adept liar.

I don't believe him. What kind of 'work stuff' involves me?

"We have dinner plans, right?" he asks.

I realize I'm twisting my hands. I force them to stay still. I need to separate myself from this man before I have serious regrets. I can't risk being alone with him again. "Something came up with my editor," I say. "We have a video call tonight. It's going to run late."

He narrows his eyes and frowns with a show of disappointment. "Really?"

"Sorry. It's important."

I retreat to my room, wanting to push all thoughts of Robert aside. Last night was wonderful, but it won't happen again. I won't let it. I can't believe how quickly I let my guard down and allowed a stranger to slip into my life.

There is no call with Donna, of course. I made that up, but I need to work. I came here to write, to complete the first draft of my novel, not fall into bed with handsome strangers who dig into my background and make suspicious phone calls about me.

CHAPTER 18

W hen my room service meal arrives, I sit at the bistro table in the corner of my suite and eat steak, a quinoa salad, broccoli, and chocolate mousse. I made the right choice by backing out of my dinner plans with Robert, yet I miss his company. I'm a little lonely, but I'm safe. Besides, my isolation is nothing compared to Hannah's. I wouldn't trade places with her for the world.

After stacking my dishes, I'm back at my laptop, ready for the next chapter.

FROM THE MANUSCRIPT

Lying on her side on the cot, Hannah stared at the notches someone else had etched into the basement wall. How long since her captor last checked on her? Twenty-four hours? More?

At home, she had three authors' manuscripts waiting for edits on her computer. If only she had her laptop, she could keep working and stay on top of the deadlines she always accepted from her boss. With all this time on her hands, she could finally write her novel. She'd always dreamed of writing a psychological thriller, but never started because she was too busy editing and polishing other people's books. Although, she could have *made* time for her work. The real problem was that her ideas and outlines never seemed good enough—the plot too complicated, the twist too predictable, the characters unoriginal. She was her own worst critic.

The truth now seemed glaring—she hadn't written her book because she lacked the confidence. She'd been too afraid to fail. Now, the opportunity might be gone.

Her colleagues at the publishing house might not even be aware she was missing. They all worked remotely. Eventually, her manuscripts would get passed on to other editors. The authors' publishing timelines would get pushed back. They'd be more concerned about the delays than her absence. Her family and Jackson were a different story. It pained her to think about what they were going through. She had to believe they would channel their anguish into making sure the police found her.

Forcing herself off the cot on unsteady legs, Hannah made her way to the bathroom to fill her empty stomach with water from the faucet. When she emerged, the streak of light coming from beneath the door filled her with dread.

Her ankle still throbbed, and the cold outdoors was relentless. The woods were his territory, not hers. Yet staying here, cowered inside the basement room, offered zero chance of escape. She could only pray someone would rescue her, but what if he tired of her first? Her gaze returned to the tally marks on the wall. The marks that eventually ended.

She had no choice but to play his game and hope it would allow her a chance at freedom. Shaking, she crept through the unlocked door and up the basement stairs. Fear seized her at the top. Was he waiting just beyond the door, enjoying her terror? She listened for footsteps or the tapping of Bolton's claws. She heard only silence, somehow worse than any noise. Where was he?

Through the cabin windows, the sky had lightened to a dark gray instead of pitch black. The sun was rising.

Bypassing the useless phone, Hannah headed straight for the fridge for sustenance. Halfway across the kitchen, she stopped. A short chain and a lock held the refrigerator door handles together. She could check the cabinets for food, but where to start? Instead, she hurried to the bedrooms in search of more clothing, only to find those doors locked, too. He wanted her outside in the sub-freezing temperatures, underdressed, weak, and starving.

Pulse racing, she fled through the front door, expecting a terrible surprise to meet her. Outside, the truck and van sat in the driveway. As she headed toward them, her foot connected with a heavy object on the porch. A gun.

Hannah couldn't tell one gun from another. She didn't know whether it was loaded or how to operate it. Her captor hadn't just dropped it there. He'd left the weapon for her to discover. How did it fit with his sick game? When she picked it up, the cold metal bit into her skin. She was afraid that if she slid it into her pocket, it would accidentally go off and maim or kill her. She held it away from her body, the barrel pointing out.

Gray morning light revealed more of her prison territory than she'd seen before. The woods were denser and more vast than she'd realized. Melting snow had left a mess of slush and mud puddles on the dirt road. Her ankle held as she hurried around them, scanning the woods for escape routes through the maze of trees, fallen tree trunks, thickly woven vines, and underbrush filling every gap.

Finally, she located an opening point, a way off the exposed road.

Every step announced her presence with loud crunching and snapping, but she kept moving. She'd made good progress until her foot dislodged a rock from under the snow. It skittered forward and vanished with a hollow thud. Hannah stopped and peered down into a massive hole concealed by dead vegetation. Not natural growth, but a deliberate trap.

Shaking, she backed away, branches clawing at her clothes.

"Move!" His voice exploded from nowhere. He was watching, had been watching, and just like last time, she hadn't heard a thing.

Terror rooted her in place. Her numb fingers prevented her from working the gun, even if she knew what to do.

"Keep moving!" he shouted again.

She dropped to a crouch and cowered, paralyzed with fear.

"You have a gun. Why aren't you using it?"

"I can't," she whispered as the weapon fell from her hand.

"Then get up and run!"

She only shook her head, huddled beneath the bushes like wounded prey, as mucous and tears froze on her raw skin.

He dragged her back, his fingers bruising her arm, cursing under his breath.

"More useless and pathetic than I thought," he said when he shoved her back into her room. "I took the wrong damn girl."

Hours later, a sound jolted Hannah from a restless sleep. Voices filtered down from above. A woman's voice. Not fearful, but furious, as if she were arguing with the man. Hannah strained to hear the words, but the walls and floors muffled the sounds, and she couldn't make sense of the conversation. She only knew she was no longer alone with the hunter.

She hammered her fists against the door. "Help! Help me! I'm locked in the basement. My name is Hannah Williams. Please, help me!"

The argument continued upstairs, but the small basement room seemed to swallow Hannah's cries. She pounded harder, and kicked with all her strength, her voice growing hoarse.

Hannah stopped kicking to listen and realized the voices had ceased. The woman must have heard.

But the silence went on. No footsteps. No one was calling her name.

She threw herself at the door one final time, screaming until her throat was raw.

No one came.

Hands bruised and throbbing, Hannah crumpled to the floor, not bothering to wipe her running nose. No one was coming. Her fear, hunger, and despair had combined into a sickness that spread through her, hollowing her out from the inside. She had so much to live for—her family and friends, the book she would start writing as soon as she got another chance, a puppy and a kitten she'd adopt from a rescue shelter, the ones that had been waiting the longest—but it all seemed so far away and unreachable, permanently pulled from her grasp. Her reality was reduced to the terrible basement room and her frail, failing body.

With those words, I prop my chin on one hand and stare out the window. Hannah's collapse should frustrate me as a writer. It's terrible storytelling to let your character give up, but oddly, I'm okay with it. It's almost as if I can't wait for her to go.

Still seated behind the desk, I scan the room, transitioning from writing mode into my real life. My empty dinner plates and glasses sit atop the console because I have yet to move them into the hallway. When my gaze reaches the closet, I remember my printed manuscript is there. I could review it before bed, but I don't have the energy. It's been a taxing, emotionally draining day. I'm a little unsettled, either from the story I'm writing or perhaps because of what happened earlier with Robert and the mysterious phone call where he said my name. At least, I think he did.

I'm torn about how to handle Robert. Should I avoid him or tell him I don't want to see him again? Both options make me uneasy and could cause awkwardness for the rest of my stay. With a sigh, I push myself out of my chair and head to the bathroom to prepare for bed. Hopefully, things will be clearer tomorrow.

CHAPTER 19

The morning passes in record time as I edit my manuscript, covering the pages with red ink, strike-throughs, and comments in the margins. When I reach the last page, a knock interrupts my work.

My initial reaction is panic. It shoots through me like an electric current. It has to be Robert, and I'm cornered. There's no escape route except the balcony, a two-story drop I'd only consider if the room were on fire and flames licked at my heels. I could answer the door and tell him I enjoyed our time together, but I need to concentrate on my book, and I'm sorry I won't be able to see him again. Or I could stay still and pretend I'm not here until he leaves.

My fingers hover above the keyboard, afraid even the softest tap might betray my presence. I'm painfully aware of how ridiculous this is. I'm a grown woman hiding in my hotel room, waiting for the person out there to disappear. I should have hung up the *Do Not Disturb* sign. No—that would only prove I'm inside.

"Hello? Ms. Williams?" The voice is male, and it's not Robert. "Are you in there?"

Who else could it be?

"I have a delivery for you. I'm bringing it in now."

This presents a dilemma. There's no time to race into the bathroom and lock the door. He'll discover me when he enters the suite. Already, I feel childish. I can imagine the headline, *Zipporah Bazile Hides from Hotel Staff*. Except I'm not Zipporah Bazile here. I'm just Hannah Williams, a regular hotel guest who can behave as oddly as she likes without fear of gossip.

Unless... what if it's not a resort employee at my door?

I spring from my chair, but I'm too late to check the peephole. An electronic beep sounds, and the door swings open.

The young man who enters is wide-eyed with surprise when he sees me. It's the University of Colorado student who transported my luggage on check-in day.

"Sorry to disturb you," he says. "I didn't think you were here. May I put these inside?"

He's carrying two bouquets: a white vase with a dozen or more red roses and a glass vase filled with colored flowers.

"Sorry I didn't come to the door," I say, trying to dispel the tension. "I was working. I didn't hear you."

"Must be a special day for you."

A special day? The date suddenly registers. It's my birthday. I forgot, but someone else remembered.

"Where should I put these?" he asks.

"The console, please," I say, noticing the small envelopes tucked into the flowers. One bouquet must be from my parents, who would never let this day pass unmarked.

I check the envelope in the colorful arrangement first. *Wishing you a day full of writing inspiration. I'm looking forward to reading your book. - Donna*

Of course. My editor knows I'm here. She recommended this resort, and she's waiting to read my draft. How could I forget?

Next, I open the card in the roses.

Happy Birthday, Zip. May your day be filled with surprises. - Robert.

Yesterday's overheard conversation clicks into place. Robert was arranging this delivery and wanted to keep it a secret.

I should have asked him point-blank about his conversation then. If he'd told me the truth, I could have enjoyed another wonderful evening with him rather than being holed up in my room with my paranoid suspicions. I can't beat myself up about it now. What's done is done. Now that I have an explanation for that mysterious call, I should feel good about us. Instead, I'm uncomfortable for a different reason.

I never told him my birthdate.

It's not public information; it's not even on my Wikipedia page. Yet, Robert is a cybersecurity expert, and learning my birthdate would be child's play for him. I wonder what else he's uncovered.

To see what online information exists about me, I turn on my laptop. First, I check my email and find a message from my parents.

We hope you're having a wonderful time and getting lots of writing done. We have presents waiting for you at home, and can't wait to celebrate with you then. Have a nice dinner with the other guests tonight. We don't want you to spend your birthday alone.

Yet here I am, doing just that. They're right. I should thank Robert for the roses and apologize for canceling our dinner. Actually, I have nothing to apologize for. He doesn't know I lied about the editor meeting. I can thank him for his thoughtful gift, and we'll see what happens from there.

As I approach Robert's door, I see it's ajar. "Robert?" I call from outside.

When there is no response, I open the door further. His room appears empty.

It's my first glimpse into his space. It has the same floor plan as my suite, with a unique personality. One wall displays a large image with leaves and pinecones. A collection of wildlife pictures hangs on the opposite wall, but I'm mostly paying attention to the details that tell me more about Robert. He's been poking into my life online, so I'm justified in having a look around.

The bed is tightly made, and his hiking boots, running shoes, and dress shoes are lined up in a neat row against the wall. Like me, he's set up a laptop on the desk overlooking the balcony. I move toward his work area, where a paper on his keyboard has neat and even handwriting, giving me more insight into his personality. As I skim it, a note in the bottom margin makes my mouth go dry. *Why are they watching her?*

I twist around at the rustling sound coming from behind me. A housekeeper emerges from the bathroom, the raven logo on her black uniform. Did I miss a cleaning cart outside?

"I'm almost finished here," she says.

"Oh, thank you." My voice sounds jittery.

I stop myself from explaining this isn't my suite and scurry back across the hall as if I'm fleeing a crime scene. As fast as I can, I unlock my door and hang up the *Please Do Not Disturb* sign. With a sigh, I sink into the armchair by the window. The words from the paper in Robert's room echo in my head. *Why are they watching her?*

The phrase could be ripped from one of my novels, from any psychological thriller. What could it mean? It's pure ego to assume the note is about me, but I can't help thinking that way. Perhaps whoever printed the Wikipedia page about me is following me around. I hope I'm wrong.

If I want to get to the truth, I'll have to ask him. No jumping to conclusions this time, yet how can I explain finding the note in his room without confessing to snooping? I don't have a way around that one.

Meanwhile, I have to get back to writing. I can't let those five haunting words derail my novel.

CHAPTER 20

FROM THE MANUSCRIPT

Hannah marked the passing of time with her growing weakness. She used to hold a plank for five minutes when she practiced yoga. Now, her shaky arms could barely assume the position. She slept, sipped metallic-tasting water from the sink, and listened to the hunger pangs groaning inside her empty stomach. When she could no longer tolerate her smell, she finally got naked and stood under the shower's weak spray until the water ran cold. When her stinking clothes became unbearable, she washed them with soap and hung them to dry. They'd grown loose and hung off her shrinking body. The day she'd heard voices and banged on the door seemed like ages ago. The bruises on her hands had faded, but no one had come to rescue her.

Hannah had lost so many things she'd always taken for granted. Safety. Warmth. The freedom of choosing what to eat and when. Her morning coffee ritual. Her daily online yoga classes. Her phone and laptop that kept her connected to the rest of the world. Most of all, she missed her parents, friends, and Jackson with overwhelming anguish. She made bargains with herself and God. She'd do anything to see them again.

Christmas must have come and gone. Her first one without her family, though she couldn't imagine they would have celebrated anything with her missing. If her captor celebrated Christmas, she saw no sign of it.

His visits followed no discernible pattern. Occasionally, he brought her food and replenished her toilet paper, soap, and towel. Sometimes, days passed with nothing but water from the sink to fill her belly.

As she did most days, she was lying on the cot, shivering from the persistent cold, when a click came from the door. He hadn't let her out to play his sick game since she'd surrendered and refused to run. This time, he didn't crack the door open and leave. Though he'd brought her nothing, he stayed, peering in on her.

"Please, let me go," she said through dry, cracked lips, wanting him to take mercy on her but also desperate to talk to someone, even him.

He remained in the doorway, ignoring her pleas and just studying her. Hannah had never felt so insignificant before.

"I need more food. And protein," she said, because he hadn't given her any protein since that first meal, and her body was failing. "Beans? You must have a can of beans upstairs."

He shook his head and left but came back with an open can of black beans. She rationed portions and eventually drank the murky juice, unsure when her next meal would come.

A day or so later, he reappeared with more supplies, a baked potato, and another can of beans.

"Do you have any books?" she asked.

He scoffed. "I don't read."

Yet later, two books landed at her feet. *The Hunter's Guide to Butchering, Smoking, and Curing Wild Game and Fish* and *Step-by-Step Guide to Making Moonshine.* She read the moonshine book first, focusing on the chemistry behind the process. The book explained the presence of all those ceramic jugs in the fridge upstairs and the liquor her captor poured into his mug that first night.

Following that, she read *The Hunter's Guide.* The images of slaughtered animals sickened her, more so perhaps because she was now someone's prey. Out of sheer boredom, she forced herself through every page.

Days crept by, and it seemed like his visits grew further apart. Each time the door opened, her heart leaped with relief, pathetically grateful for any contact and whatever food he brought her. The fear of abandonment now overshadowed her fear of him.

When clumps of her long hair began to fall out, a consequence of cheap shampoo and malnourishment, she sat cross-legged on the cold floor, weaving the long, brittle strands back in the way she used to braid her horse's tail.

"Deep into that darkness peering, long I stood there wondering, fearing."

Muttering lines from Poe's *The Raven*, she wondered how long a person could endure psychological and physical abuse. How long until she completely broke? Would she even realize it when it happened?

Huddled against the damp wall, knees pulled to her chest, she heard him coming. The sound of his footsteps triggered a giddy sense of relief after her endless hours of solitude.

He unlocked and opened the door to toss a granola bar onto the floor. "They have these at work. I don't like them. Figured you would."

"Thank you!" Starving, she crawled on all fours to snatch the bar. As she tore open the wrapper, she asked him the question she'd been holding onto for days and days. "Someone was upstairs. What happened to her?"

Hannah worried her screams had condemned another innocent woman to a fate perhaps worse than captivity.

"Nothing happened to her. She didn't hear you, and she left." He sneered. "That was a long time ago. Trust me, no one is ever going to find you here."

"My family will," she whispered, more to convince herself than him. "They won't stop until they do."

"Doesn't matter if they never give up, they still won't find you. I've told everyone there's no trace of the missing woman, that whoever took her must've crossed state lines on the 77 and vanished. Around here, people trust their sheriff."

His words severed the thin thread of hope that remained.

"You don't look so good, Hannah. I don't think you'll make it much longer. You're just a useless, broken doll no one wants to play with."

She curled up smaller and covered her ears, unable to endure any more of his cruelty. Hannah had reached her breaking point. Her vision blurred as she retreated deep inside herself, seeking shelter in the darkest recesses of her mind.

Poor Hannah. Her entire life, she's been surrounded by love and unwavering support from her family and friends. She's never faced any hardships or pain. When I put her in this situation, she never had a fair chance. Now, she's trapped in an endless cycle of fear, never knowing if he'll return or leave her to starve alone in that basement. The psychological anguish has depleted her, stripped away her hope, leaving her barely human.

She's not the fierce survivor readers expect from my other novels, and the time has come to end her. She needs to be erased. Again, for reasons I can't explain, her demise brings me an unexpected sense of satisfaction.

CHAPTER 21

I n the morning, I reread the last parts I wrote, then edit until I'm no longer making the writing any stronger, just different. I have to stop revising and get on with the next chapter, but I have a problem. I'm stuck. I've had enough of Hannah's suffering, but I'm uncertain what to write next.

To reset my creativity, I peruse a list of articles about miracle products and superfoods, scrolling and clicking and only partly absorbing the details. By late morning, my eyelids are drooping. A nap would be wonderful, but I'm not ready to give up on writing my next chapter yet.

Until this point, the story just flowed out of me, but something has changed.

Pacing my room doesn't help. Nor does stretching. When I return to my desk, I've still got nothing. Absolutely nothing. No inspiration. No direction.

Waiting for the perfect idea isn't a good strategy. I've given that advice countless times. Usually, I force words onto the page and rely on tomorrow's editing to sort the good from the mess. It's better to have any words at all than to face the taunting glare of a blank screen. Yet today, I can't follow my advice. It's a challenge to come up with anything new. Hannah's tormentor has pushed her to the edge, and her endless cycle of abuse can't continue. This should be the beginning of her end, but I'm not sure how she should die. She can't just fade away, can she? That's not interesting enough. I let out a heavy sigh. This shouldn't be so hard, but it is.

I need help, so I call my editor.

"How are you?" she asks, her voice calm as always.

"I'm well. The resort is wonderful, just as you said. Very quiet and beautiful."

"I agree. I'm glad you're appreciating it. Where are you?"

"I'm in my suite."

"How is the book coming along?"

"That's the thing; that's why I called you. I guess I'm looking for a pep talk. It *was* coming along fine." I bring her up to speed with a high-level overview of what I've written so far. "And now I'm stuck. It's driving me nuts, the being stuck part."

"If you'd like, you can send me what you have so far. I'll read it over and give you some feedback."

"Sure, that might help. I'll send it."

"After you send it, why don't you get out of your room and take a hike? Enjoy the resort."

I nod, though she can't see me.

After copying everything I've written into a Google doc for Donna, I look out the window. A couple passes by with backpacks and hiking poles, inspiring me to take Donna up on her suggestion. I lace up my hiking boots, grab my pack, and head outside.

The overcast sky matches my mood. I slip on sunglasses from habit rather than necessity.

Before hitting a trail, I stop in the lobby for some recommendations.

"Good afternoon, Ms. Williams," the manager says.

"Good afternoon," I answer, impressed that he remembers me from the check-in.

"How is your stay so far?"

Images flash through my mind: mysterious granules swirling in my coffee's foam, my Wikipedia page abandoned on the printer, the strange message in Robert's room—*why are they watching her?* Without proof of anything and with my true identity hidden, there's nothing to say, no crimes to report, only minor and unrelated incidents. It's not as if someone here is stalking me.

"Everything is wonderful," I lie. "Can you suggest an intermediate hiking trail? Two or three miles."

"The *Pine Ridge Trail* is a favorite for hiking. It's a little over two miles."

"Any other options?"

"*Glass Lake Loop* is more challenging. It's three miles long. There's a waterfall and lake at the halfway point."

"That sounds good."

"Most hikers complete it in ninety minutes. It's well marked, but here's a trail map, just in case."

His smile lingers a beat too long. Does he recognize me? Or has gossip about my nights with Robert circulated among the staff? The thought makes my cheeks warm, though Robert and I are hardly having an illicit affair. As Hannah Williams, no one should care what I do or who I do it with. Surely, I'm one of countless single guests who have hooked up with a random stranger here.

My thoughts drift to Robert. I wonder what he's doing now.

With a goodbye wave for the manager, and the trail map folded inside my small backpack, I leave the lobby and head to *Glass Lake Loop*. I should be back long before it gets dark.

Thick clouds block the sun as the trail disappears into the dense woods before me. Even on a cloudless day, there wouldn't be much sunlight coming through the tree canopy. I pluck my sunglasses off and slide them into my pocket so I can see where I'm going.

Often, I do my best thinking when I walk. Once I've established a comfortable walking rhythm, I turn my attention to Hannah's situation.

"Maybe she starves to death. Dies of hypothermia. Or he shoots her," I mutter. There are only so many ways to die. Which one best suits my story?

I'm completely lost in my thoughts when a twig snaps behind me. I jerk around, but the trail is empty. The sound must have come from birds or squirrels.

I continue along, considering different possibilities under my breath, trying to flesh out the next critical chapters of my novel. The trail grows steeper, and the light perspiration across my forehead and between my breasts becomes a dripping sweat.

When I break for water, I'm shocked to discover two hours have passed. The trail never looped, and I never saw a lake. I must have missed a turn. After gulping water, I unfold the map and try to figure out where I am.

The resort's trails—hiking, skiing, horseback riding, biking—travel like brightly colored arteries and veins across the paper. According to the map, I should have curved back toward the resort long ago. I could retrace my steps, but that means two more hours in growing darkness. Through the trees, the sky has turned a menacing gray. A storm is brewing.

To keep from panicking, I consider the obvious facts of my situation. I'm at a luxury resort armed with a map and a phone. I'm not lost in uncharted wilderness. One call and the resort can send an ATV to get me. I like that idea, so I pull my phone out. A "No Service" message displays on the screen.

Another sound makes me whip my head around. "Is anyone there?"

I resume walking as fast as I can, pumping my arms, my face screwed into a hellbent expression I can't control. I'm certain someone is out there. Maybe the same people Robert mentioned on that paper I found. It could be a photographer who discovered my presence and began stalking me, hoping I'll pee in the woods so he can plaster humiliating images all over the Internet. I do have to go, but I'll hold it.

When I find the loop again, my relief is short-lived, vanishing when a deafening crack of thunder erupts above the trees. Rain hammers down, turning the trail to a muddy soup. I break into a jog, head bowed against the deluge, feet sliding treacherously beneath me. With no warning, my legs sweep forward, and I crash down, mud coating half my body.

As I stare up from the ground through a curtain of rain, a figure in neon athletic wear materializes. It's Sarah. She's not muddy, but she's equally drenched, her usual friendly smile replaced with concern.

"Oh, dear. Look at you. Let me help," she says, extending her hand.

I scramble up, wiping my muddy hands on the front of my shirt. "Were you following me?"

"No. Just out for a hike." A slight smile returns to her face, but there's something off about it. "I didn't expect this downpour," she says. "We should head back before it gets any worse."

We rush along the trail, heads down against the driving rain. Her presence is comforting because I'm no longer alone, but also unsettling because I think she was following me.

Around the next bend, the woods open to reveal the main lodge in the distance. Sarah heads for the gym, claiming she has dry clothes there, but the awkwardness between us lingers. She must realize I suspect her. Why was she out there? Is she just a lonely traveler seeking a connection with another person traveling alone? Or is she a reporter who's discovered my identity and is now gathering material for an exposé?

Or is there another reason, a truth I can't yet see?

CHAPTER 22

After getting lost, drenched, and muddy on the trails, I'm like a bedraggled rat who just climbed out of a sewer. I want to get inside my room before anyone else sees me like this.

Naturally, the first person I encounter is Robert.

He stands in the Elk Lodge corridor, his workout clothes clinging to him like a second skin, accentuating his physique. Unlike me, he prepared for the weather and carries an umbrella.

A contagious smile spreads across his face as he takes in my sopping clothes and hair. "Don't believe in umbrellas where you come from?"

I shrug and squeeze water from my hair.

"I skipped my trail run because of the rain. Now I feel like a lightweight," he says.

I wrap my arms around my sodden torso, covering my chest. "There's still time to redeem yourself."

He laughs. "A treadmill will be fine for today."

I remember the note I found in his room, but this isn't the time to get into it. I'm still unsure how to explain finding it. Fortunately, I also remember the reason I went to see him. "Oh, I stopped by your room earlier to thank you for the flowers, but you weren't there. That was very thoughtful of you."

"My pleasure. I was worried they hadn't come. I hope you like roses."

"Yes, for sure. I love roses." The air is thick with unspoken tension between us. I'm desperate for a hot shower, but after that, I'd like to enjoy dinner with him and figure out the meaning of that note. If all goes well, I wouldn't mind another night together in my room. I attempt to convey all that with a single look.

"Are you planning to work on your book again tonight, or would you like to have dinner together?"

My telepathic process worked, yet he's offering me an easy out. Nice.

"I'd love that. Eight o'clock?"

"Perfect. I'll pick you up." He laughs at his joke. We're literally across the hall from each other.

In my suite, I peel off my wet and muddy clothes. In the shower, I shave my legs with more care than usual until my skin is smooth. I'm excited about more than just dinner. All it took was seeing Robert and his smile. Any worries I had about him are gone.

Our table beside the giant stone fireplace in Raven's Watch Tavern is cozy and elegant.

I snap a few photos of the fireplace, trying to capture the true essence of the resort for later. When I finally turn away from the flames, I find Robert watching me with an appreciative look.

Everything on the menu tempts me, and I'm eager to try something different, like steak from the resort's herd of cattle or elk from the mountains around us.

We've just ordered our wine when Robert takes out his phone. "I stumbled onto something interesting." The gleam in his eyes tells me he can't wait to share what he's found. "Your publisher released a statement about your upcoming novel."

He didn't just "stumble" upon it. He's been searching. Part of me wants to stop him from telling me more, but curiosity wins.

"They're calling it a psychological rollercoaster. Your most shocking work yet," he says.

"That's standard publisher hyperbole. They profit more from my books than I do. They have to say those things."

Robert isn't finished. "*Whispers of Darkness* continues Zipporah Bazile's acclaimed series. In her newest, Katya Straus teams up with psychiatrist Dr. Evelyn Rice. Driven by a desire to understand Katya's past, Dr. Rice finds herself entangled in a situation that threatens her safety."

Unease spreads through me like a glass of spilled red wine. My fingers curl into fists by my sides as Robert continues.

"It wouldn't be one of Bazile's novels without a mind-bending twist. With her uncanny ability to tap into the darkest corners of the human psyche, she explores trust, betrayal, and the fragility of the human condition. *Whispers of Darkness* is destined to become another bestseller."

Robert finishes reading and focuses on me.

I force a small, shaky smile as a rush of adrenaline makes me dizzy. The story he just described is completely foreign to me. It's not the novel I'm working on. I'm not writing another book in my *Darkness* series. Katya isn't part of it, and there's no character named Evelyn Rice.

"So, Katya is your heroine? Tell me about her," Robert says.

Completely distracted by the information he just shared, I answer with a mechanical response pulled straight from my website's FAQ section. "Katya is a special agent and the protagonist in my bestselling series. She's resourceful and unstoppable. She finds solutions when the odds are stacked against her, when everything is on the verge of falling apart. She's a little unconventional with her methods but has a heart of gold."

"Katya sounds like someone I'd like to meet."

"That's what my readers always say, and after writing thirty *Darkness* books, I know her well. She's like my oldest and closest friend." That last line is part of a quote, also listed on my website.

"Interesting. It makes sense that she seems real to you."

Our conversation pauses while the sommelier pours wine. When he leaves, I ask, "Where did you find that press release?"

"Goodreads. They're featuring your novel as an 'upcoming thriller to watch for.'"

That's terrible. Goodreads is a popular platform for devoted readers. Thousands of them eagerly await my new releases. Due to this mix-up, they'll be expecting a story they aren't going to get.

Robert is oblivious to my discomfort. He's still in a good mood. "I thought you said you didn't have a title yet."

"Guess I do now." I take a giant gulp of wine. "Sometimes the publisher chooses my titles." I'm just making things up as I go. I'd never let anyone choose my title without consulting me first, but I don't want Robert to see how upset and confused I am.

The server returns for our orders, but my head is spinning. How could this awful mix-up have happened?

CHAPTER 23

After our dinner, we decide to try the outdoor hot tub. I hope Robert's company will temporarily take my mind off the mix-up with my current novel. I've already sent Donna a text message about it. I'm anxious to check the Goodreads article for myself, but Robert is standing in the hallway, waiting for me to grab my bathing suit.

I fidget as we order cocktails, then follow separate paths through the changing rooms before reuniting outside on a stone patio. Dark silhouettes of the mountain peaks form the backdrop. Strands of tiny white lights thread through nearby trees. It's a beautiful resort, and I should try to appreciate that more while I'm here, especially now that I'll have a lot to deal with once I leave. I can't imagine how to straighten the misunderstanding about my new book.

The water is too hot at first touch, but once I'm submerged to my shoulders with my lower back against a pulsing jet, the temperature seems just right.

I raise my drink in a silent toast, then take a few generous gulps. I'm tense. I need to get rid of the sick feeling in my stomach and relax. That should be my priority. Everything else can wait.

Robert stretches his arms along the tub's edge, his profile turned toward the mountains. From this angle, his face is unfamiliar. Suddenly, again, I'm uncomfortably aware of how little I know about him.

When he turns to me, I say, "The night we met, you said you needed to get away. What from?"

His lips tighten, accentuating the tiny lines around his eyes. "I went through a really difficult client situation."

"What happened? If you don't mind talking about it."

He sighs. "The project wrapped up over a year ago. We identified vulnerabilities, presented findings, laid out worst-case scenarios in explicit detail, then gave our recommendations."

I slide over a few inches, letting the jet find a new pressure point on my back, drawn into his story. "And?"

"The client ignored our recommendations. Months later, they got hacked, exactly as we'd predicted. The CIO tried to blame us."

I arch my eyebrows. "He accused you of the hack?"

"That or passing the idea along." Robert's jaw tightens. "Baseless accusations, but their legal team made destroying us their mission. Our lawyers cleared us, but it was an exhausting, expensive ordeal."

"So, you didn't do it?" I tease.

Robert jerks his head back. "No, Zip. I don't create problems to fix them. I don't need to. My company has more legitimate work than we can handle."

"Just joking. Sorry. It's all behind you, though?"

"Finally. I'm more selective with clients now. If they don't intend to follow our recommendations, there's no point finding their vulnerabilities. Having said that, if it hadn't happened, if I hadn't needed a break, I wouldn't be here with you."

He moves toward me, closing the gap between us. Our eyes meet and we kiss. When we part, his gaze lingers on my neck. "You have a mark here, below your ear."

"My birthmark. It's like a tiny paw print, isn't it?"

With a light touch, his fingers trace my birthmark. Even in the hot water, his contact sends a pleasant shiver through my body. Each caress intensifies the pull between us.

His hand slides lower, between my legs. The tub is extra steamy until voices intrude on our bubble.

We separate as another couple comes around the corner.

I realize my glass is empty, my mouth is dry, and the heat is getting to me. "I'd better get out and cool down."

Robert takes my hand, helping me out of the tub.

Back in my room, we find each other again. His touch is gentle but confident, a little familiar, yet still thrilling. I arch into his embrace, wanting more.

Afterward, wrapped in his arms under the sheets, I'm content and don't want to move a muscle. I mull over the ups and downs I've experienced since meeting him. It could be the wine in my system, combined with my complete satisfaction, but my suspicions and irritations now seem absurd. I'm almost ashamed. It's like I was actively trying to sabotage my happiness. Thank God I didn't succeed.

Just before drifting off with Robert's hand wrapped around mine, I let myself imagine this relationship has real potential, if I can completely trust him.

With no warning, a voice inside me whispers, "Do you think you can trust him? What happens if you continue this relationship beyond the resort and let him see who you really are?"

I stir from my sleep and open my eyes to a faint light. A shadowy figure moves near my desk. Why is there someone in my room? Then it dawns on me—it's Robert. That understanding brings comfort for only a few seconds. The light is coming from my laptop screen. He's sitting behind my desk, at my computer.

"What are you doing?" I ask, pulling the sheets over my chest.

He turns around. "I couldn't sleep."

"Why are you over there?"

A few beats of tense silence pass before he answers. "Just thinking."

He crosses to the bed and wraps his arms around me. The embrace should be comforting, but I can't relax now. I'm not hugging him back. "What woke you?"

"Anxiety." He chuckles, but I can tell he's serious. "I have an early work meeting. Still have prep to do."

"What time is it?"

"One-thirty. I should have done some work earlier, but I was having too good a time with you. I do my best work late at night, anyway. Sorry I woke you."

His lips brush my forehead. It's a sign of affection rather than lust. If I hadn't found him awake at my desk, I'd find it comforting.

"I better get going," he says. "Go back to sleep, and I'll see you in the morning, okay?"

He slips out of my suite, leaving a trail of questions in his wake.

Why was he moving through my room while I slept? What was he doing at my computer?

CHAPTER 24

When morning arrives, I'm cozy under the sheets and duvet. Then I remember last night, and finding Robert awake by my computer, and I'm chilled again. My trust issues return in full force.

My entire life's work is on that laptop, including my current manuscript. Until it's released to the public, it's private, especially in this unfinished draft state. It's only for my editor and me.

I took a risk being intimate with someone I may or may not trust. I don't know Robert well enough to decide which it is. That is the problem.

I throw back the covers, swing my legs over the side of the bed, and pad toward the bathroom. The shower spray tempts me to stay under long after I'm done cleaning up, as if enough hot water could wash away my doubts. So many things feel off. The stalled progress on my novel, the erroneous Goodreads article, which got me so flustered I forgot about the strange note I found in Robert's room. And most bothersome—Robert at my desk in the middle of the night.

Wearing the resort's thick robe, I call Donna. When she doesn't answer, I leave another message about the Goodreads article mix-up. With that done, I plop back in bed and scroll through the latest news stories on my phone. I'm procrastinating rather than facing my manuscript.

I march over to my desk, determined to write. A slip of hotel notepaper beside my laptop stops me.

I didn't want to wake you, so I'm leaving this note. Unfortunately, I have work to do before the morning. Thank you for another wonderful evening. I can't wait to see you tomorrow. This is my phone number: 809-422-5806.

I let out a low whistle. One mystery solved. Robert was writing a note. While he was doing that, he must have bumped my laptop and woke it up. If only he'd mentioned the note last night, he could have spared me a lot of worry. I'm glad he left his number.

Reassured, I log into my computer and check my inbox. There's an email from Donna that opens with, *Don't worry about the press release you saw. I'll handle it.*

Another relief. I just hope it's not too late.

She's also read my manuscript and sent me a list of suggestions, all focused on my main character.

- *How would you describe Hannah's emotional state?*

- *How do you envision her character evolving during captivity?*

- *In the subsequent chapters, can you elaborate on her coping strategies?*

I appreciate Donna's guidance, but these suggestions aren't helpful. There is no more evolution for Hannah. I need one final hurdle between her breakdown and death, a flash of defiance to make readers love her before I break their hearts. Then I'm going to kill her off.

I reply, *Thanks for the feedback. I'm planning to have Hannah die in the next chapter. Not sure how yet. I'm still suffering from writer's block.*

Donna's response is almost immediate.

NOT a good idea. DO NOT kill Hannah! It is not an option for this story. You'll alienate readers. Find a creative way for her to get out of there alive.

I'm stunned by Donna's response. It's totally out of line, a mandate rather than an editorial suggestion. Since when does she tell me what to do? This isn't her novel. It's mine. If I choose for Hannah to die, that's what's going to happen.

I roll my eyes for good measure, but deep inside, warning bells are clanging.

I have four hours until my massage appointment. More than enough time to knock out another chapter. Hours pass, yet my word count only shrinks. I'm still editing, revising sentences that probably don't need changing, but not writing anything new to move the story forward. Neither the ideas nor the words are there for me. I can hardly believe I've got writer's block, but I do. I'm just sitting here wasting precious hours. Finally, it's time for my massage. I leave my room and walk across the resort.

The spa is all gentle music and flickering candles. I try their specially blended hot tea, and it's pretty good. After a few minutes, Heidi, my masseuse, leads me to a room scented with balsam and vanilla. She leaves the room while I take off my clothes, and soon I'm face-down under a heated blanket, resting my head against a firm, round opening.

As I wait, I contemplate the problem with my novel. I could abandon the dark tale entirely and start fresh with a new story using Raven's Hollow as the setting. Three couples, dark secrets, mysterious murders. A locked-room mystery instead of a psychological nightmare.

Heidi taps the door and asks, "Are you ready?"

The room dims, and my massage begins. Under her skilled touch, the tension in my neck and shoulders loosens. The rhythmic kneading dissolves my worries. I'm floating along, enjoying the soothing sensations.

With little warning, everything changes, and my eyes snap open. Not from anything Heidi has done, but from something within me. A vague but urgent idea claws at my consciousness, jarring me from my relaxed state and requiring my full attention. It's there, just under the surface, but I don't want to let it in.

I turn around and sit up, my nerves suddenly on edge. Pressing my fingers against my temples, I fight the sensation until it's gone.

"Did I hurt you?" Heidi's concerned face comes into focus.

I shake my head, clutching the blanket to my chest, more confused than her. I have to get out of this small, dark room. "Everything's fine," I stammer. "I just remembered I have an urgent matter to attend to."

"You still have thirty minutes."

"Sorry. I have to go. It was wonderful. Thank you."

I've offended her, but I'll leave an enormous tip to compensate. I wasn't lying about the massage. It was wonderful until it wasn't. Something happened or was about to happen to me. I don't understand, and I can't explain.

Later, while getting ready for my dinner with Robert, I keep thinking about the troubling sensation that interrupted my massage. The high altitude could be responsible, or a hallucinogenic in the spa's specialty tea. I'm aware that's ridiculous, and it's not the first time I've worried about someone tampering with my beverage here. I just wish I had a better explanation. Any explanation.

CHAPTER 25

As we navigate through the Ranch House Restaurant, Robert touches my shoulder, and I loop my arm through his, anchoring myself in his solid presence. I squeeze his hand, and he squeezes back.

Musicians provide live background music by a wall of windows. With Robert's hand in mine, I focus on the sound, separating it from the hum of intimate conversations around us.

After the sommelier pours a deep crimson liquid into our wineglasses, we raise them in a toast.

"To our time together," Robert says, "may it be as exciting as one of your novels."

"I love that toast. I'll drink to that."

Robert sips his drink, then takes out his phone and places it on the table. "I have to show you a picture I came across. I got a big laugh out of it. Take a look." He slides the phone toward me.

After the Goodreads article, I don't want any more surprises, but maybe this is different.

An image of a beautiful woman with long legs fills his phone screen. She's lying on the foredeck of a yacht, wearing an unbuttoned white shirt over her navy bathing suit. Long black hair streams out from under an enormous sun hat. The photo has a too-perfect quality that makes me think it's an advertisement.

"Is this your next vacation destination?" I ask.

"Nope. Read what it says under the picture."

I lift the phone closer and read the caption. *The elusive Zipporah Bazile sunning on a yacht in Greece.*

"Obviously, that's not me. I'm here with you," I say, sliding the phone back to his side of the table. "That's what I get for eluding the public. The media can convince people that nearly any Caucasian woman with long black hair is me, and no one except my family and close friends can say otherwise."

"Will you or your publicist correct them?"

I trace my wineglass rim and smile. "Why should we? The woman is stunning. I'm fine with being mistaken for her. Those legs." I widen my eyes to emphasize I'm impressed.

"Not as nice as yours," Robert says, which is an excellent response.

"You can't trust anything you read online about celebrities. Almost all of it is pure BS. Please don't waste any more of your time searching."

Robert's smile shuts down as I replay that last bit. It didn't come out quite right. I sounded more severe than I intended.

A server approaches, carrying our appetizers. It's excellent timing, and I'm grateful for the distraction.

We eat in silence until I try again, lightening my voice and changing the topic. "I had my massage earlier today."

"Good. Did you enjoy it?"

"Yes." I don't explain that I enjoyed it until the moment when I couldn't bear another second. I still don't understand the source of my panic. "Did you drink the specialty tea in the spa when you were there?" I ask.

"The tea? Yeah. It was good. Did you?"

"I tried it before my massage. Did it make you feel unusual in any way?"

He studies me before answering. "No. Why?"

"No reason." There's probably nothing to it, so I keep my suspicions to myself and change the subject yet again. "I'm going horseback riding tomorrow."

He tilts his head, studying me again. "You ride?"

"I used to ride every day when I was a child and through college. Why do you sound surprised?"

"I'm not," he tells me, but the look on his face says differently.

"What about you? Any hobbies? Sports you play?" I ask, though I think I've asked him that question already. I can't remember the answer.

"Tennis and golf."

"Oh, right, right. I knew that. Sorry."

There's a forced quality to our conversation. It's a major disappointment. Perhaps a few cocktails at the bar will reset our mood.

We leave the restaurant together with space between us, not touching or holding hands.

Robert's phone rings. He checks it and accepts the call. "What's going on?" he asks in a low, serious tone I have yet to hear until now. Placing his phone against his chest, he turns to me. "I have to take this. Sorry."

"Of course." I wander across the lobby, studying the rustic artwork. Vintage maps hang beside wilderness scenes painted in earth tones, but it's the antler chandelier that triggers an unsettling sense of déjà vu. Like I've stood here before, in another life. The same unsettling sensation from the massage room hits me, like there's an idea trying to surface. I'm consumed by a desperate need to escape, yet I don't understand what I'm running from. Something unusual is happening—these episodes of almost-remembering. I can't decide if I should tell Robert what's going on, or if I'll sound like a nutcase.

I head into the gift store and drift through the aisles in a daze, selecting and purchasing candles with the raven logo for Donna and my parents. When I return to the lobby, Robert is still on the phone, his brows pulled together.

I want to be near him, drawn by my attraction but also the need for comfort. When he finishes his call, I'll tell him what I experienced, vague as it is. Perhaps he'll help me sort it out. I'm still wishing I hadn't snapped at him earlier, but I can make it up to him so he'll forget it ever happened.

When he finally lowers his phone, he's frowning. "Work situation. Not what I planned for tonight. I'm so sorry. I have to deal with this."

I can't bear for our evening to end on an uncertain note, like so much else in my life recently. Taking his hand, I say, "I understand. Do you think it will be an hour? I can wait."

He hesitates, then shakes his head. "I'm unsure how long it will take, and I don't want you waiting up for me. But tomorrow?"

I nod. "Tomorrow."

Trying to reestablish our rapport, I snuggle against him as we walk back to Elk Lodge. I'm still hopeful he might change his mind, and his work issue can wait.

"Sorry to ruin our night," he says again when we reach the corridor between our rooms, and I realize I'm going to bed alone.

The kiss I give him is deep and desperate. When he kisses me back, pressing his body against me with his fingers in my hair, I think everything might be okay between us.

By the time I enter my suite, I'm convinced an early night and a good sleep are best for me.

CHAPTER 26

After a great night of rest, I'm still unsure how to move my novel forward. It's not for lack of trying, but I'm stuck and distracted. I place part of the blame for that on Robert and last night's abrupt ending. I haven't heard from him yet. Maybe he's still working, pulled into an all-night crisis.

The sky is blue, and there's no rain in the forecast. It's a good day for horseback riding, and Robert and I could go together. He seemed skeptical of my riding experience, and I'd love the chance to prove him wrong. Excited about the prospect of an outing with him, I send a text.

He replies promptly, and I'm a little annoyed as I read his message. *Sorry. I have to work today.*

There's no warmth in his response, no suggestion of rescheduling or making plans for later. It seems like a curt dismissal. Still, I rationalize. There's a chance he was on a work call and only had a second to respond.

Determined not to let his response derail me further, I head out alone. Passing Robert's door, I picture him on the phone at his desk, dealing with whatever crisis emerged, because that's what I want to believe. For his sake, I hope it's not another difficult client or a lawsuit.

By the number of people out and about, I seem to be the last one at the resort to start my day. I'm passing by the fitness center when I see a sight that stops me cold. It's Robert. He's talking to a curvy woman in a powder-blue sundress. He's not working.

I watch from a distance as the woman pushes her brown hair to the side, and I realize I know her. He's with Sarah.

They're not touching or holding hands. She's focused on him with a curious intensity, asking him questions like she's giving him the third degree. Robert isn't my boyfriend, but we've been intimate, and we've spent so much time together. It's normal that I'm a little territorial.

I veer away without trying to get Robert's attention. Betrayal overshadows my breakfast. I only eat a few bites of my omelet because my appetite is gone.

When I reach the stables, the man working there asks about my riding abilities.

"I've ridden most of my life," I tell him. "But give me a horse with a dependable personality. One I can trust. I need that today."

He laughs, though I'm only partly joking. "They're all pretty sweet and dependable. We have a group trail ride in a few hours."

"I'd rather go now. Alone. I'll stick to the trails. You don't have to worry about me. I promise I'll be fine."

He finds a helmet my size and watches while I saddle and bridle a chestnut gelding named Roger. Ten minutes later, I'm off, determined to forget about whatever Robert and Sarah were doing and make the most of my day. The trail opens to stunning views, just what I needed to put things in perspective. For twenty minutes, I'm relaxed in the saddle, thinking about my story until I'm jerked from my thoughts. A scream erupts from the woods.

Roger snorts beneath me. I pat his neck, trying to soothe him and myself as I scan the area.

Eventually, I urge Roger forward again. Minutes pass in tense silence until I hear voices and a muffled cry, this time closer.

Gulping down my fear, I guide my horse off the riding path and onto a walking trail, toward the sounds and into a clearing. The scene there makes me gasp. A woman cowers on the ground, face contorted in pain, while a man towers over her. There's an object in his hand. He's about to hurt her. Suddenly, I'm no longer seeing strangers but Hannah and her captor.

"Get away from her!" I shout, coming straight toward him.

The man stumbles back, confused, as he opens his mouth.

"Leave her alone!" I shout again.

"Stop!" the woman yells, lifting her palms toward me. "He's my husband. He's helping me."

My heart races as I realize I may have misinterpreted the scene. I was certain the woman was in danger. "I heard screaming," I say, my gaze moving between them. "I thought you were hurt."

Clutching the man's arm, the woman says, "I twisted my ankle. We've called for help already, but thank you for caring enough to stop. It was brave of you."

I study their faces, unsure if I believe her. They're both staring back at me like I can't be trusted. It's now clear I imagined a scenario that doesn't exist.

"I could give you my horse," I offer.

"Again, thanks, but it's not necessary. The resort's sending someone."

"I'm sorry," I say, for lack of anything better.

I'm embarrassed by my reaction, though I was just trying to help. My imagination sometimes gets the best of me, causing me to see things that aren't there. I need to get back to writing and channel those dark ideas into the pages of my book where they belong.

CHAPTER 27

With two yanks, I close the balcony curtains against the glare before sitting down at my desk. Pulling my chair closer, chin resting on my hands, I stare at the last sentences I wrote in my manuscript.

"You don't look so good, Hannah. I don't think you'll make it much longer. You're just a useless, broken doll no one wants to play with anymore."

She curled up smaller and covered her ears, unable to endure any more of his cruelty. Hannah had reached her breaking point. Her vision blurred as she retreated deep inside herself, seeking shelter in the darkest recesses of her mind.

What comes next?

I grasp my hands in my lap, and avert my gaze from the scene I just can't seem to build on. This is like having insomnia, tossing and turning in bed while the minutes tick away. The more I concentrate on the next chapter of this story, the more it eludes me. I've never hit a wall like this before.

There's also Robert's silence. I haven't heard from him since I saw him with Sarah. I'd like to know where we stand, but I'm not going to chase after him. I won't contact him again.

My resolve to ignore him lasts less than a minute. I grab my phone and fire off a text message. *Horseback riding was great, by the way. You should try it sometime.*

I wonder if my sarcasm will come through. Either way, it's too late to take my text back now.

Little dots float across my message screen. He's typing a response.

I thought you were terrified of horses.

His reply makes no sense.

I want to respond with, "Is that what Wikipedia said about me? It's common knowledge the site isn't always accurate." But the less I say, the better. If things end badly between us, he could post my responses online and embarrass me in public. I need to take the high road, or I might regret it later. There's no doubt I'm truly confused about him.

I set my phone down so I can get back to writing. Seeking inspiration, I pull *Her Darkest Lies* from the books I brought. When I open the front cover, I find an inscription I did not expect. *To Emma W., I'm glad you're a big fan. Thank you for your support. Zipporah Bazile.*

The inscription is a reminder that my readers are counting on me. I've promised them a new novel, and I must deliver. The pressure is real when deadlines and expectations are looming.

I also wonder why I didn't give this book to Emma. Did I sign it, then notice an error with the copy and give Emma another instead? Yes, that's probably what happened. My supply of author copies has arrived with flaws in the past.

As I flip through the pages of *Her Darkest Lies,* the characters and plot twists come rushing back to me. I've written so many books. Why am I stuck now? Why can't I figure out Hannah's trajectory?

There's something wrong with me. Something I don't understand.

My phone chirps, so I turn it over. It's Robert. After seeing him with Sarah when he said he was working, I'm half-expecting an apology. That's not what I get.

Can we have dinner tonight? I need to discuss something with you.

Considering our limited communication recently, it can't be a good thing. But why bother with a discussion over dinner if he's done with me? We'll soon go our separate ways. If he's lost interest, there's no reason to see each other again. He could simply avoid me for a few more days and be done with it.

My active imagination goes to work, conjuring discussion possibilities. Until I find out what he wants to discuss, I won't be able to focus on much else. I can't wait until dinner.

I hit the bathroom to brush my teeth and apply lip gloss, then head across the hall. My knock goes unanswered. "It's me," I call through the door. "Got your text."

I'm about to leave when I hear, "Hey, just a minute. I'm coming."

I stand there for at least ten more seconds, wondering what could take so long. Finally, he opens his door and invites me inside.

He's half-naked, a towel wrapped around his waist, but his hair is dry. Am I interrupting? Is there another person here? My thoughts go to Sarah.

I scan the suite. The bathroom and closet doors are open and the spaces are unoccupied. There aren't many other places to go unless she's out on the balcony or hiding under the bed, waiting for me to leave.

My thoughts make me cringe. My paranoia and distrust continue to grow like an open and infected wound, intent on spreading. I can't stop it from happening.

Robert tilts his head toward the bathroom. "I was just getting in the shower. Can you give me a few minutes, and I'll be right out?"

Under different circumstances, my timing might have led to a nice opportunity to join him, but there's nothing seductive about his question now. He neither smiles nor frowns. The look he gives me makes no sense. I've not seen it before, but if I had to guess, I'd say it's sympathy.

What does he have to tell me? Did he download and read one of my *Darkness* books, and now he's spooked?

Robert retreats into the bathroom and closes the door behind him. I hear the lock turn, which is unexpected, considering we completely explored each other's bodies in my room. I'm left alone in his suite, feeling like an intruder. At least this time, I didn't sneak in.

His wallet lies on his desk alongside his laptop and a few papers. I should leave it alone, but his last strange note made me curious enough to justify looking.

I hear the water running behind the bathroom door as I cross the room and flip his wallet open. A few credit cards are slotted inside, with an American Express Platinum card on top. A Seattle driver's license confirms his identity. There's nothing unusual inside. I close the wallet, making sure it's right where he left it.

Confident I have a few more minutes to poke around, I scan the papers on his desk. The top one contains notes—some full sentences, others mere fragments. I read a few lines, and blood drains from my face. Baffled, my eyes flick to the top of the page, and I read the content again.

Abducted from a rest area in NC. Her boyfriend didn't see it happen. Held captive in a remote area of the mountains for five months. Hunted for sport. Psychological and physical abuse. How does she escape?

The paper quivers in my hand. These aren't just random notes—they're the meat and bones of my story. A story I've never shared with him. How did he get this information? And why would he want it?

I regret not digging into his background the way he dug into mine.

The shower cuts off. My gaze flies to the bathroom door, and I hurry out.

In the hallway, I instantly regret leaving his notes behind. I should have taken everything with me and read more.

My entire body is shaking.

What the hell is going on?

Who is Robert Yates?

CHAPTER 28

Taking long strides on a path beneath a canopy of trees, I grapple with my discovery. I still can't believe I found the outline of my story in Robert's room. What a fool I was for trusting him. I ignored so many red flags, blinded by his charm. I convinced myself I was being unnecessarily paranoid. He's not the person he pretended to be. Was any of it real? He's probably not an IT consultant but an author or journalist trying to scoop my story. I can't count on anything he told me. How could I have been so gullible?

With each step, my regret deepens. Beyond my embarrassment, there could be legal matters to consider. I should call Donna for guidance and find out if we have to call my publisher. Yet, before I call anyone else, I need to speak with my father. I can count on him to help me through this.

He picks up my call right away.

"Dad? It's me. Can you talk for a moment?"

It must be the tone of my voice because his immediate response is, "Are you all right?"

"Yes, for now." I lower my voice, though the trail is empty. I still can't escape the feeling I'm being watched.

My mother's voice comes from the background. "What happened? Is she okay? Where is she?"

"I'm walking on a trail at the resort, and I'm okay, but the retreat isn't going so well. Something creepy happened."

"Tell us, dear. We can help." Her voice is stronger now. They've put me on speakerphone.

"I met someone my first night. Robert. He seemed like a nice guy, but now I think it was all an act. I think he stole my story."

"Okay. Slow down," my father says. "What story?"

"My new one. The one I came here to write. I told you about it. The main character gets abducted from a rest stop and is held captive by a psychopath. Remember?"

"Yes, of course. I remember it well."

"I found notes on a paper in Robert's room. Plot points nearly identical to my novel."

A few beats later, my father responds. "Is it possible you told him what you were writing?"

"No, definitely not. I haven't told anyone except you, Mom, and Donna. He's a professional cyber hacker, supposedly. There are so many ways he could have accessed my files. He might have hacked into my laptop through the wireless connection here."

To preserve my dignity, I don't tell my parents I shacked up with a stranger and that Robert was in my room and had access to my laptop while I slept. Admitting that means I have terrible judgment in choosing who to trust. But that's most likely when he stole my story. Getting past a simple password would mean nothing to someone with his skills.

I groan when I realize Robert might have a digital copy of my entire manuscript. This is turning into an epic disaster.

"Did you confront him?" my father asks.

"No. I didn't say anything about it. I was too shocked. After I found the notes, I left before he saw me."

A branch snaps behind me. I spin around, ready to shout at whoever is tailing me, but the trail is empty.

"First, let me look into Robert," my father says. "What's his full name?"

"Robert Yates. He's from Seattle. In his mid-thirties. And Dad, I think he tried to drug me a few days ago. I left him alone with my coffee, and when I came back, I saw something that didn't belong there. I didn't drink it." I consider mentioning the strange feeling I had during my massage after drinking the tea, which also made me suspect I might have been drugged. Did Robert have something to do with that?

My mother lets out a mournful wail. "Oh no, I told you—she should just come home."

Before I can ask why she said that, my dad cuts her off. "Why didn't you tell us when it happened?"

"Because I wasn't sure, but now, all these strange things are adding up one on top of another. I should have been more careful."

"Don't worry," my father says, his voice softening. "If you want to come home tomorrow, I'll book your flight."

"I should. I wanted to finish my rough draft, but I can't focus. Too much is happening."

"Don't force it, honey," he says. "You don't have to. Let me handle everything. You just try to relax."

"Thanks, Dad. I love you. You're the best. You too, Mom."

"We love you too, Dear. Immensely." His voice cracks on the last word before the line goes dead.

My mouth opens in surprise. I could have sworn he was choking up as if he were crying. That's not like my father at all. Is he that worried? Do I sound completely unhinged, and I don't even know it?

CHAPTER 29

After a long walk alone, where at least I didn't get lost, drenched, misinterpret anyone's behavior, or get followed by Sarah, I return to the resort. I'm on high alert, checking out my surroundings with every step, wary of crossing paths with Robert. I should probably confront him, but not until I learn more about who he is and why he took my story ideas.

When I get to Elk Lodge, I peer into the corridor, scanning its length to make sure he's not there. Seeing it empty, I slip in like a spy creeping into enemy territory. I try not to make a noise as I open my door and step inside. Just as quickly, I bolt the door behind me.

My gaze roams the suite and my belongings. The space became mine for a few days, but now it seems contaminated. I can't stay any longer, not with Robert across the hall. My father suggested I leave early, and I'm tempted.

I grab the room phone and jab at the front desk button. A woman answers, and I picture the young lady who has now helped me several times in the lobby.

"Hi. I need to switch rooms." My voice sounds strangled. I cough to clear it.

"Is there a problem with your current suite?"

I rally an excuse that won't raise questions and draw more attention to myself. "There's a problem with the hot water."

"I'm sorry about that. We can send maintenance right away."

This is turning out to be harder than I thought. "No. The air conditioning isn't working properly either. I just need a different room."

A knock comes from my door. Please let it be housekeeping.

"Zip? It's me. Robert."

I hold my breath, afraid to move.

The desk clerk continues speaking. "I'm looking for another suite we can move you into right away. Give me just one moment."

I hang up without saying a word.

"Zip?"

Every fiber of my being tenses as I pretend I'm not here.

"Zip, please. I know you're in there. Open the door."

My heart pounds, but I stay quiet.

"All right, just hear me out. I care about you. A lot. I want to work through this. We can talk about it."

Work through what? Is he aware I found the notes about my book? Or is he talking about whatever he might have going on with Sarah? I don't ask. I keep my mouth shut, barely breathing.

"I'm not upset with you, just confused. I'm sure you have an explanation."

My mouth falls open. Did I hear him correctly? *He's* not upset with *me*? I rack my brain, searching for what I could have done wrong. He violated my trust and stole my work, yet he speaks like he's uncovered some dark secret about *me*. This is the definition of gaslighting. I've written about it before, and now it's happening. Luckily, I'm too aware to fall for it.

Robert continues talking from the corridor. "You haven't been truthful about some things, but it's okay."

What is he talking about? I hid my identity at first, but he already told me he understood. Didn't he?

"Leave me alone," I finally blurt. "Or I'll call security. The police."

"Why would you do that? Why don't you want to talk to me anymore?"

I clench my fists by my side. "I know what you did. I saw your notes. You stole my story."

He doesn't respond right away. Maybe he's trying to think up an excuse. "You think I stole a story? What story?"

His tone makes doubt creep in like a frigid draft under a poorly sealed door. Could there be another explanation? No, this is manipulation at its finest.

"Look," he says, "you've got me very confused. I'm not sure what sort of game you're playing, if that's what this is." He pauses for so long that I think he might have left. "But I want to understand you, if you'll let me."

My resolve wavers. Despite my concerns, I must understand why he jotted those notes on my story and what he thinks is "going on" with me.

I should shut him out completely. He's caused me so much worry and confusion already.

I shouldn't let him in.

I won't.

"Zip?"

My hand trembles as I unlock the door.

CHAPTER 30

A s soon as I turn the lock, I back away, clutching my phone.

Slowly, the door opens. Robert hesitates in the doorway before stepping inside. The door clicks shut behind him.

Trapped, I walk backwards toward the wall. Without looking away from Robert, I tap my phone screen to make sure it's awake and ready so I can summon help if needed.

Robert stays by the door, one hand hidden behind him. His tender expression throws me. It's not what I expected, and if it's an act, it's very convincing.

His hand emerges as he takes two steps forward. He's holding a piece of paper. "I wish you hadn't found those notes in my room. I didn't mean for you to see them."

"Obviously not." My anger gives me courage. "Those were my story points. My ideas. Why would you take them? Who are you?"

"I'm exactly who I told you I was."

"Why should I believe you?"

He sighs. "Because why would I lie?"

I let out an incredulous huff. He's trying to make me sound like the unreasonable one. "You lied to get close to me so you could steal my story."

Robert shakes his head. "Those notes you saw—I didn't steal them from you or anyone else. Please, just look at this." He holds up the paper in his hand. On it is an image of a woman with long, dark hair. "I just printed this. Look at it, please."

"You won't stop digging, will you? Is that another fake photo of me? Where am I now, hiking the Appalachian Trail?" I plant my hands on my hips, feigning a confidence I don't have. "You need to stop researching me. Stop Googling me. Stop showing me pictures. Just stop." I mean what I say, but I can't resist a peek at the photo.

I edge closer and recognize the person in the image. It's either me or my doppelgänger. The way she's standing, the tilt of her head, her hairstyle, her clothes—they're all different, yet she has my eyes, my nose, my chin, my exact hairline with a widow's peak. She has my birthmark.

"I'm sorry for making you uncomfortable." His gaze moves to the photo. "But you know who she is?"

I throw up my hands. "What kind of question is that? It's me," I say, though I'm not entirely convinced that it is.

He nods. "I thought so. Then again, I also thought you might have a double out there. Did you see the caption?"

My gaze drops to the text beneath the image. There's a name there. *Emma Wilson.*

"Is Emma Wilson your real name?" Robert's voice is gentle, not accusatory.

"No. I don't know any Emma Wilson." A memory flickers, then fades as I utter those words. The name is familiar to me. It's from the inscription I saw earlier. The note I wrote in *Her Darkest Lies*. "To Emma W."

Confusion reigns inside my head. I signed a book for someone named Emma W. Someone who could be my twin.

I don't understand what's going on.

CHAPTER 31

My thoughts are spiraling out of control. "Get out," I tell Robert as I point at the door with a shaking hand.

Someone used photo editing tools to alter that photo. They took my face but changed the clothes and hairstyle and added my birthmark. Did Robert do it? Why would he? Is he angry that I lied to him about my identity when we first met? If this is a revenge mind-game meant to leave me utterly confused and vulnerable, it's working.

Robert is still standing there, watching me. He hasn't moved. He's got a pleading look in his eyes. What on earth is he after?

"I care about you, but we have to be honest with each other." He rakes his fingers through his hair, then gazes up at the ceiling for a few seconds as if he can't express himself. "I'll go, but if you want to talk, you know where to find me. I'm here for you."

"I would very much like you to go." I point to the door. I need time to change rooms and get as far away from him as possible.

He places the photo on the console table. "I gave you my phone number. Call me or knock on my door when you're ready to talk. If that's what you want. I'll be waiting."

Only after I close the door and slide the bolt into place can I breathe properly again. For the past day, I thought Robert was ignoring me. Instead, he occupied himself with stealing my story and stalking me online.

What's his agenda here? This Emma person could be part of it, an obsessed superfan who crossed a line into dangerous territory.

I need to call my father again. I hope he's uncovered things about Robert that will explain everything.

My father answers my call instantly, as if he's been waiting. I tell him what happened with Robert and how it's left me shaken. "Have you found out anything about him yet?"

"I haven't, but I'm working on it. Can you sit tight for a while longer? I'll get back to you soon." It's not a dismissal. From the concern in his voice, anyone could tell how much he cares about me and how worried he is. He's going to help me.

"Sure. I'm sorry to bother you with this, it's just I'm so confused. I don't understand him and it's freaking me out. I'm trying to move to another room. He's right across the hall, and I don't feel safe anymore."

"I'm sure you're safe there. Please don't worry." At the same time, I hear my mother in the background saying, "Tell her not to worry. She's safe. She should lie down and relax."

"Tell Mom I can hear her, and I will. Please call me as soon as you find something."

An odd loneliness sets in once we're off the phone. I trust my father to look out for me, but I can't wait. I must do something. I turn to my laptop to uncover the truth about Robert.

He never told me the name of his company. I type *Robert Yates, cyber security,* and *Seattle* into the search bar and find it. CyberStrike Assessments. After clicking the website link, I navigate to the company's list of security experts. Robert's headshot, with the words *CEO and founder,* dominates the top of the page.

So far, he's legit. He didn't lie about what he does for a living. He's a cyber security specialist. Everything checks out with his career and company, which only leaves me more confused.

Cyber security. Cyber hacking. The more I ponder his skill set, the more disturbing my history with him becomes. I unknowingly invited a professional hacker into my room while I slept. It shouldn't surprise me if he's already privy to every detail of my life. Yet, why target me? Why would he care about my books? And what does he think I've done?

My thoughts fly back to the day we first met when we walked to the restaurant at the same time. Our accidental encounter, his innocent and charming smiles. Which of us suggested drinks that night? Was it him or me? The details blur.

Robert always seemed to be in the corridor whenever I was there. Not every time, which was clever of him, because that would be a dead giveaway. Just often enough to pass for random chance. I frown, strumming my fingers atop the desk. None of our encounters seem like lucky coincidences anymore.

I don't recall grabbing a paper napkin off my desk, but it's in my hands, and I'm mechanically tearing it into shreds, the tiny pieces falling like confetti against my leg. When I scoot my chair back and pick them up, something about the action is familiar. It's another flash of déjà vu, but I can't afford to chase the vague memory now.

I need to learn the truth about Robert, and I won't stop there. He's not the only one involved.

I also need to know who Emma Wilson is.

CHAPTER 32

I'm so stressed that my ears are ringing when I finally type *Emma Wilson*.

The first results puzzle me. A handful of photos and some locked social media profiles. Emma guards her privacy as carefully as I do. Perhaps she's also famous.

I keep clicking. There must be more. I notice a pattern in the dates. All her social media activity stopped last year. Nothing since then. No posts, no updates.

When I find an article with her name on it, I hesitate. Do I really want to find out who she is? Learning about Emma enables her to invade my thoughts.

The article's headline surprises me. *Local Woman Missing. Emma Wilson was last seen with her boyfriend, Jackson Porter, at a highway rest area.*

Already, the parallel between Emma's ordeal and my manuscript is impossible to ignore. After stealing my unfinished novel, Robert must have scavenged for ideas online and come across Emma Wilson's story. But why stick her name on an altered photo of me? Merely to confuse me?

I return to reading and find more. After five months of captivity, travelers found Emma in terrible condition. A few more days and she might not have lived. They took her to the hospital, and from there, she went home with her family. And that's it for her story. There's no mention of a dramatic rescue or a heroic escape. Nothing about her abductor's capture.

I search for further information, but I can't find anything else. Even if I wanted to draw from Emma's ordeal to complete my novel, the parts I need aren't there. The climax is missing. How did those five months end? How did Emma get away? Did someone eventually find her—the police, a search party, a knight in shining armor?

Perhaps the truth was too terrible to print, but, since when does the media hold back disturbing information? If anything, in this age of sensationalism, that's what sells ads and articles. The only plausible explanation is that the information isn't out there because no one knows the truth. No one except Emma. She'd have to know.

If only I could interview her. After what she endured, she has first-hand experience and knowledge I can use to fuel my ideas. I could even say my story was inspired by a true crime. I doubt she's the same Emma I signed my book for, but if she is, surely she'd be pleased to meet me. I consider asking my agent to set up an interview, but it's insensitive and inappropriate. Especially since the real-life Emma survived, and my character will die.

With a sigh, I close my internet browser and return to staring at the last chapter of my unfinished manuscript. My ending is waiting for me somewhere. I just have to find it.

Before I can figure out how my protagonist meets her end, there's another knock at my door.

CHAPTER 33

The knock comes again. It must be the hotel staff coming to help me move. My gaze roams the room, assessing what I have to gather up and pack into my suitcases. My stomach is in knots from the drama and stress around me. Robert better not follow us, or I'll have changed rooms for nothing.

Before opening the door, I peer through the peephole.

"What the heck?" I'm so surprised, I just stand there, blinking and looking again, unable to trust what I see. For the second time in less than ten minutes, I am utterly bewildered.

My parents are in the corridor. It seems impossible, but they're out there.

I wonder if I'm dreaming all of this. I just spoke with them twenty minutes ago. How are they in Colorado, so far from home in North Carolina?

"Honey, it's us." My mother's voice carries through the door. "We're here."

In a daze, I open the door to face them. I'm too shocked to do anything except gape.

My mother wraps her arms around me. "Oh, sweetheart."

I hug her back, stammering, "Wow. This is a surprise. Why are you here?"

"To help you." She releases me but still holds onto my arm. "We checked into the resort a few days after you did. We were worried about you."

"I don't understand. Why would you be worried about me?"

I'm sure it relates to Robert. He's done something awful. Whatever they uncovered must be worse than I can imagine.

My father places his hand on my shoulder. "There's something we have to tell you. It will help explain the confusion you're experiencing. Maybe you should sit down."

I remain standing. "What is it? You're scaring me. Please, tell me now."

He continues in a flat tone, which I recognize as his sad voice. "In the past, you endured something painful over a long period. So painful, your mind couldn't handle it."

I frown at him, then laugh. "What? No, I didn't. I would remember."

"You may not remember, but it happened," he says. "To cope, your brain formed another identity to protect you. It's called a dissociative disorder. That's what you have."

The term registers. I know what a dissociative disorder is. I've read about cases. It's a split personality. Multiple personalities.

My gaze darts from my father to my mother. I'm waiting for them to tell me they're joking, but they don't.

"What are you saying?" Fear makes my voice sound strange, like it belongs to someone else. "You came all the way to Colorado to tell me I've got mental health issues because of an ordeal I don't remember? And I have another personality I'm not aware of?"

My father's slow nod sends the room spinning. It suddenly seems too small for the three of us.

An inappropriate laugh escapes me. The concept of having another personality is too bizarre to comprehend. Wouldn't I feel it? Wouldn't I know? It can't be true. "That's not possible," I say.

"It's true," my mother answers.

Driven by morbid curiosity despite my disbelief, I narrow my eyes and stare back at them. "If I have another personality I don't know about, who am I when I'm not me?"

My parents exchange a look as if they're afraid to tell me.

"That's not the right question to ask," my mother says. "The thing we need you to understand is that you're not who you think you are."

My mouth hangs open. "Huh? You're going to have to explain."

She takes my hand. "You're not Zipporah Bazile."

I shift away from her. "That makes zero sense. What are you talking about?"

"You're not a famous author. You're an alter-personality for our daughter."

"What do you mean, *your daughter*? *I'm* your daughter."

My mother shakes her head. "Our daughter survived a horrific ordeal. In order to cope, her mind fragmented into another personality. That's what you are. You're her alter-personality."

CHAPTER 34

M y parents just told me I'm not who I think I am. I'm not Zippo-rah Bazile, a bestselling author. I'm someone's alter-personality. Essentially, I'm not real.

They've lost their minds.

"If I'm not your daughter," I say, shivers running down my spine, "Who is?"

"She's an editor at New Relic Publishing," my father answers. "Her name is Emma Wilson."

Speechless, I clutch at my chest. My thoughts are fuzzy, and I have an urgent need to flee the room and hide somewhere. They're telling me I'm an alter-personality for someone named Emma Wilson. That's the name beneath the photo Robert showed me.

"That's absurd," I finally say. "I'm Zipporah Bazile." I gesture to the *Darkness Series* books I brought along. "Those are mine. I wrote them."

"They're your books, but you didn't write them. You purchased them." My father enunciates as if he's speaking to a frightened child. "Zipporah is your favorite author. You've read all her books. She even signed some for you. Look inside the covers."

When I don't move, he takes the copy of *Her Darkest Fears* from the shelf and opens it to the first page.

There's another inscription there. *To Emma W., thank you for being a huge fan. I'm sure you'll publish your first book soon. Get writing! - Zipporah Bazile*

A terrifying chill runs through me. There are inscriptions to Emma W. inside not one, but two of my books. How can that be? How? Then I understand. Robert must have written those lines while I was sleeping. And the photo of me—he could have easily put the name Emma Wilson on it. Those things are simply further evidence I'm being manipulated.

I grin because I can't help it, I'm so freaked out. What they're telling me is preposterous. I know who I am. The question is, why would they make this up? It's one thing for Robert to mess with me, although I don't know why he is, but my parents' betrayal terrifies me. Who can I trust if not them?

Maybe it's all a misguided joke. Is it April fools' day? No. But all this could be part of a twisted celebrity prank show. I need to get veto power over the footage so none of it goes public. There's nothing amusing about my shock and confusion.

My parents seem so sincere while begging me to believe I'm not who I think I am. I didn't know they were good actors, but nothing else makes sense. These are the same parents who were excited about my writing retreat. They encouraged me to come here.

In defiance, I lift my chin to present an excellent point. "If what you say is true, why pretend until now? Why let me believe I'm someone I'm not?"

My mother grimaces as if she's experiencing the pain of a dozen hornet stings. "We're so sorry we did that," she explains, tears in her eyes. "When Emma left, and your personality suddenly emerged, the doctors thought you could help. They thought writing would heal Emma."

"Heal her from what?" I ask.

"Her abduction and captivity," my mother answers. "The trauma she endured last year."

"Excuse me, but what are you talking about?" I ask.

My mother pressed her hand over the base of her throat. "Someone abducted Emma from a highway rest stop and held her captive in a remote cabin. Does that sound familiar to you?"

"Yeah, it's my story."

"Exactly," she says. "The story you're writing isn't fiction. All of it happened to Emma."

I stagger backwards as bizarre laughter bubbles up from deep within me. Once more, I can't believe what I'm hearing. "Come on. Now you're telling me the manuscript I'm currently writing, the one I'm creating chapter by chapter, isn't fiction?"

"It's not." Tears roll down my mother's cheeks.

I shake my head so vigorously it makes me dizzy. "You want me to believe that I'm not me, I'm someone named Emma, and the manuscript I'm writing isn't fiction because it really happened? Any other bombs you want to drop on me?"

My mother lowers her gaze. "The powder in your coffee. That wasn't Robert. We asked the barista to add your medication. You weren't supposed to notice."

"You did that?" I ask, horrified. "You tried to drug me?"

"We love you no matter who you are," Dad says, pleading, "But we want our sweet Emma back. We want her to get better."

"We need our Emma back." My mother's words dissolve into sobs. "She's in there somewhere, and she has to come back."

This is insane. There's no Emma inside me. I am Zipporah Bazile, a renowned author, and for some frightening and mysterious reason, they're trying to trick me.

I retreat further into the corner of my suite and finally sputter the only words that come to me. "I don't believe you."

CHAPTER 35

M y parents finally leave me alone. I close the door to my suite behind them, silencing their apologies and professions of unconditional love. My skull throbs as I drop my head between my hands. Am I losing my mind?

I'm a writer. I create dark stories with powerful twists, but what they've told me is beyond the limits of my imagination. It can't be true.

In case it's all a sick prank, I spin around, searching each corner of the ceiling for cameras filming all of this. Surely that would be illegal, wouldn't it?

There's nothing obvious hanging on the walls, so I examine each object, running my fingers over the picture frames and the coffee maker, checking for tiny camera holes. Still nothing. It occurs to me that Robert, a security expert, might have surveillance equipment so small I'll never find them. If he's in on this, he could have installed tiny cameras while I slept.

On the shelves, one of my books, *Whispers of Darkness,* has fallen to the side. That's right, *my* books. I wrote them. Every dark setting. Every twisted character, and the good ones, including Katya Strauss, my courageous heroine, who deals with each obstacle I throw at her and always comes out ahead of the villains despite the odds.

I cross the room and place the paperback upright again. If this is a prank, those inscriptions are incredibly clever details.

Unwilling to remain in my room and continue questioning my sanity, I cover my hair with a scarf, put on my sunglasses, and head into the corridor. As I walk, I keep my gaze straight ahead. I don't want to see or interact with anyone else.

I can't believe my parents are here at the resort, yet they didn't tell me. They spied on me. They tried to put medicine in my coffee! Their betrayal is disturbing and bizarre. They claim I'm delusional, but they're the ones with the problem.

Outside, as I walk on the paths, I glance behind me. Now I'm sure people are watching me. How many here are part of this plan to trick me? There must be a film crew. A producer and a director. Sarah might be one of them. I better get my act together in case I'm being recorded. I can't let people see how upset I am. I keep my chin held high as I ascend the steps to the main lodge.

A small fire dances in the center fireplace inside Raven's Watch Restaurant. They've set the tables for the evening meal, but the chairs are all empty. There's no music. An unsettling silence has replaced the laughter and conversations that previously filled the space. It's almost surreal, and I wonder if there's any chance my entire day, or even my entire previous week, is part of an odd, vivid nightmare.

A nearby clanking sound makes me jump. It's just a resort worker moving crates on a wheeled pushcart, but it shows how on edge I am.

My footsteps quicken, taking me deeper into the main lodge. The movie theater is empty and dark inside, so I slip in and take a seat in the back. With my head in my hands, I sit where there's almost no light and hidden cameras can't get usable footage of me.

My phone has several text messages from my parents. *Please don't be angry. We love you. You are our world, and we would do anything for you. We all hoped this might work.*

They're continuing this bizarre and frightening charade.

What bothers me most are the doubts creeping in. Is what they said possible?

And what's with 'We all hoped?' We who? Does that include Donna, my agent? She recommended this retreat. I have to call her now. I need to talk to someone who will assure me I'm all right and I'm the person I've always been—Zipporah Bazile. As ridiculous as that conversation will seem, it's necessary. Once that's accomplished, I'll figure out what to do about my parents.

CHAPTER 36

The scent of buttery popcorn permeates the theater. Air conditioning hums in the background, although it's much too cool already. Goosebumps prickle my arms.

Gripping my phone, I glance around. Rows of empty seats line the large room. It looks as if I'm alone, which is what I wanted. I'm still wary, half-expecting someone to crawl out from under a seat with a camera and flash and snap a photo of my shocked face.

I don't want Donna to pick up on how frazzled I am. Remembering the yoga instructor and all the fuss about breathing, I shut my eyes and take slow inhales and exhales for what seems like minutes but might only be seconds.

Donna is a very busy woman, and I'm grateful when she answers.

"It's Zip." I speak just above a whisper. The theater might be empty of people, but there could be hidden listening devices.

"Hello, Zip." Donna sounds as calm and composed as ever. She epitomizes professionalism. "Your parents just left me a message, and I'm concerned."

I'm shocked they called her, and I should probably apologize, but before I do, Donna continues. "I was hoping you would call. Please give me some time to wrap up what I'm doing so I can call you back. I'd prefer a video call. Where are you now?"

I glance around the dark theater. "In the movie theater at the resort."

"You should head back to your room so we can talk in private. It won't be more than twenty minutes."

"Okay. Sure."

"I'll get back to you soon," Donna says before our connection dies.

She's right about going back to my suite for privacy. There can't be cameras there, or they would have caught me naked coming out of the bath. They would have captured everything Robert and I did in bed. Imagining sex tapes of me going viral brings a sour taste to my mouth. It's just too much on top of everything else. It would be one hundred percent crossing a line that no film crew could cross. No, Robert might have installed the cameras after the second time he stayed overnight. I didn't find any evidence of cameras, but what do I know about high-tech surveillance equipment? I need to check again, more thoroughly this time.

I head for the privacy of my suite, wondering what my parents told Donna and what she's thinking. She'll probably suggest my mother and father need psychological help. Unless this is a big, not-at-all-funny, horribly distasteful prank. Despite my disgust and disapproval, I'm praying that's what it is.

Back in my room, I scour every inch again, standing on chairs to study every crevice of the walls and crawling on my hands and knees to check under the furniture. I discover dust bunnies under the bed. Nothing more.

When I'm finished with my search, I'm feverish and out of sorts. I hover over the toilet bowl, taking gulping breaths, expecting to throw up. That doesn't happen, and my nausea remains. I comb my hair and dab blush on my cheeks. My hand quivers when I apply my tinted lip gloss. Color smears above my lip, making one side of my face resemble The Joker. Given all that just happened to me, it's odd to focus on my appearance, but I need to have control over something. I don't want to look as frazzled as I am.

The seconds tick away. Twenty-five minutes pass. I keep checking the time.

Donna calls a few minutes later. It's not a video call, as she mentioned, but a regular call. So much for fixing my makeup. I answer immediately. "Hello. Thanks for calling me back."

"Are you in your room?"

"Yes." The sound of her voice is soothing; it's a familiar comfort in my life.

"I was worried," she says.

"Because of my parents? They told you what they told me?"

"Yes. That must have been a very upsetting conversation for you."

I can't help but laugh at the absurdity. "It all came out of nowhere. And that's after processing the surprise that they're here at the resort. What else did they tell you? That they think I'm someone else?"

"Emma Wilson."

Hearing that name again makes me shiver. "Right. That's what they told me as well. In hindsight, I can think of several things I should have said, but in my shock, I didn't handle it well. I should have mentioned you, for one. Because why would I have an editor if I'm not a writer? And you recommended I come here to write."

"I suggested the resort because it's safe. We thought writing the story might help Emma heal, and she would come back to us."

Wait, what? My blood freezes as I replay her words in my head. Emma again. Why does she keep coming up?

"I apologize for not explaining this to you earlier, Zip. The truth is, you are not a famous author. You only believe you are. In reality, you're exactly what your parents explained. You're Emma's alter-personality."

Hearing this again from someone else is too much. Shock vibrates through my body like radiation, intent on poisoning me. I have to lie down. I stare at the wall opposite my bed. A painting with horses and cowboys blurs into indistinguishable colors. My fingers clench the edge of my phone. A cold sweat breaks out on my skin.

"Are you still there?" Donna's calmness seems so wrong with the chaos unraveling around me.

"What did you say before?" I finally utter.

"Your parents weren't lying to you. I'm not your editor. I'm your psychiatrist."

I'm clenching my jaw. I can't breathe.

Donna continues, her voice unwavering yet empathetic. "I've been working with Emma for a year. A man abducted her and held her captive in a secluded cabin. There are things she can't remember, important things about how she escaped. We've been through so much therapy, all to allow her to remember, face her trauma, and move on. I suggested she write about her ordeal, as a form of treatment. We were finally making progress, but I must have pushed Emma too hard. She suddenly left us. She fractured. That's when you emerged."

I gulp, unable to believe what I'm hearing.

"You seemed to have no awareness of Emma, no idea she existed, yet you were ready to write her story. You thought it was fiction, but it's not. What must be confusing for you is that we encouraged you. We believed you exist to help Emma cope, and that finishing your current manuscript, remembering what happened, is the key to making her whole again."

"I sent you my story, and you sent me editorial comments," I say.

"I apologize for not telling you the truth. For playing along with your delusion."

"I am Zipporah," I hiss, the words escaping my lips in defense and desperation like a snake's venom. "I've always been her."

"I know you believe with one hundred percent certainty that you are Zipporah Bazile, but I promise you're not. You're an alter-personality of Emma Wilson. You're part of her, and you can't stay in control indefinitely. Your presence is causing confusion for you and those around you. Emma needs to come back."

My mouth still hangs open, and my throat is dry. Never have I felt so empty and alone. I slap my cheek, then again, certain this is a vivid nightmare. I don't wake up, and the pain is as real as my confusion.

Ever since my arrival at Raven's Hollow, it's been one weird occurrence after another. And now this. How can this situation get any worse?

CHAPTER 37

Donna keeps talking in that calm, professional voice that never falters, but I can't listen. It's all I can do not to shout at her.

I'm off my bed now, clutching my phone, pacing back and forth in my suite. If only I'd never come to Raven's Hollow. I wish I was back home in my office, surrounded by things that belong to me and represent me.

"Emma has family and friends who love her and care about her more than you could ever imagine," Donna says. "They've been there for her every step of the way. Even at Raven's Hollow, they've been keeping an eye on her. Sarah is Emma's closest friend. She arrived on the same flight as you and stayed until Emma's parents arrived."

I let out a loud huff. I always thought there was something suspicious about Sarah. "I've never met that woman before arriving here, but I knew she was following me. And what about Robert? What's his story?"

"Robert? Is he a staff member at the Lodge?"

"You tell me."

"I don't know who Robert is. I understand this is extremely difficult, but please try to stay calm. You have a meditative app to help with that. Do you see it on your phone?"

"An app won't help me calm down, Donna. This is a little bigger than that, don't you think?"

"Let's talk about how you're doing."

Donna's soothing voice only makes me angry. A bitter laugh erupts from deep within me. "Well, I've just been told that I have two personalities. How do you think I'm doing? It's *great* to be told that you're delusional."

"What you just said, it's not entirely correct."

"So, now I'm *not* delusional?"

"You are, and that's not unusual, considering what Emma endured. Her disassociation is a normal response to an unbearable situation. The brain will do whatever it can to keep from shutting down. You are Emma's protective coping mechanism."

"So, I am delusional," I say, growing angrier. "Then what did I say that wasn't correct?"

"About the two personalities."

"Meaning?"

"There's at least one more alter-personality in Emma. She has three."

A sickening wave of dread washes over me. I don't believe any of this, yet I want to crawl out of my skin and hide somewhere safe. Somewhere these unfamiliar "others" can't find me.

"How do you know?" I ask, though I'm afraid to hear the answer.

"Emma is a sweet and gentle person."

What's the significance of that statement? Is she implying that I'm not?

"I started treating her a few days after her release from captivity. She remembered everything about her ordeal until a point. She truly doesn't know how she escaped."

"Maybe this Emma person you're all obsessed with didn't get out and ended up dying there."

"She did not die." Donna's tone leaves no room for argument. "Emma can't account for days before she escaped. One possibility is that her brain repressed the most traumatic parts of her ordeal. However, my professional opinion is that she separated herself from her abuse by developing another personality, and she isn't aware of what that personality did when it was in control."

Despite myself, I can see Donna has all the makings of a psychiatrist rather than an editor. That knowledge, added to everything else, makes me dizzy. I sit on the bed again. What she's telling me is frightening, yet it makes sense. It could happen. All of it is possible, I suppose. Of course, it is. The possibility is scientifically and medically proven, and I'm an open-minded person. I believe it. I just can't believe or accept it happened to me.

Every muscle in my body is tight to the point of snapping. "The problem with your theory is that I have always been me and no one else. I'm sure of it."

"I understand you feel that way, Zipporah, but remember the Goodreads article you told me about? It described Zipporah Bazile's next book. It wasn't the book you're writing."

"The media gets things wrong all the time."

"And consider this—you wrote the first chapters of your manuscript with relative ease. Once your main character reached her breaking point, you've had trouble continuing the story."

"Writer's block is normal. Especially with distractions. I've had a lot of those."

"It was easy for you at first because your subconscious accessed Emma's memories of her abduction and captivity to write your novel. You were writing about what happened to Emma. Now, those memories have run their course."

"That's not true. It hasn't been easy to write this book. I've had to dig deep to create every sentence."

"I don't imagine it's been easy to structure the story, to choose the right words and create the pacing, but everything in your novel represents a variation of events Emma has recounted in our therapy sessions. Everything you've written matches what she's already told me. The basement room. The hunting episodes. Her malnutrition and despair. Even the tally marks, the socks, and the beans. It's what happens next that Emma hasn't told us. I believe she can't tell us because she doesn't know. And you don't seem to know either."

Donna's response sends another shiver down my spine, deeper and colder than before. She's right. The story was there for me, and then it wasn't. I'm having trouble coming up with the rest.

After what Donna has told me, I believe I know the answer to my next question, but I muster the courage to ask it, anyway. I have to be sure. "Why would Emma's memories stop at a certain point? Why didn't she remember escaping?"

"Because it wasn't Emma who escaped from captivity. And it wasn't you, Zip. It was someone else."

"The third personality you think is somewhere inside me?"

"Yes. Another personality is aware of what happened in that cabin when Emma disassociated. We need to discover that truth for Emma. It's what will allow her to get better and move forward with her life."

It's too hard to believe what I'm hearing. I laugh from deep inside, and the sound of it frightens me. "If this other alter-personality knows what happened," I say, mocking Donna, "I'd be grateful if he or she finished writing my novel for me."

The mockery vanishes, replaced by an icy cold wave of terror. What if an entity inside me answers that challenge? What if someone else is in here, waiting for an invitation to emerge?

CHAPTER 38

After my jaw-dropping conversation with Donna, my legs are weak, and it's hard to breathe.

My phone buzzes as I sit on my bed. It's my parents. I can't talk to them. I send them a message instead.

Please leave me alone.

Continuing to dwell on the matter can't be good for me. It can't be healthy. I need to focus on the things in my life that remain untouched by this madness. That leaves me with almost nothing.

I get up and splash cold water over my face, then load a dark brew K-cup in the coffeemaker. I'm already jumpy and light-headed, my nerves frayed.

As I walk to my desk, carrying my coffee between trembling hands, I spill the brown liquid, staining my shirt.

My unfinished book hangs over me. I have to complete it. Or do I? Are readers waiting for my novel? What if there *is* another version of Zipporah Bazile somewhere—on a yacht in Greece—living a life I couldn't fathom? Is she working on a new Katya Strauss novel, the one Goodreads is so excited about? I don't know what is and isn't real anymore. Robert's involvement remains unclear.

Finishing my story might be the key to everything, a way to get myself back on solid ground.

Seated at my laptop, I press my thumbnail into my cuticles so hard a drop of blood appears. I stare at the manuscript on my screen, still deciding what should happen. Hannah is near breaking, and circumstances have handed me a powerful new idea. An alter-personality could emerge and help her get out of there. But how? What could an alter do that she couldn't?

The alternative is to kill Hannah as originally planned. She's nothing more than a character I created. I can eliminate her. Yet, as much as I want to, I can't.

Gripping the neck of my shirt, I rock back and forth in my chair. What is wrong with me? Am I completely delusional and I'm not Zipporah Bazile at all, but an imposter in Emma Wilson's body? What if I've never even written a book before?

I open my browser and search for Zipporah Bazile. The first link directs me to Wikipedia. I hold off for several heartbeats before summoning the courage to click.

There's more emptiness than information on the page. It doesn't even have my birth date. When I found the printed page in the business room, I only read the first few sentences before I tore the paper up, but now I take it all in. Most of the information is dedicated to my books, the awards they've won, and the film and TV adaptations that followed.

Then I see it. *Strange Facts.*

A single sentence makes me sag into my chair as coldness spreads through my body. *After almost getting trampled by a horse when she was six years old, Zipporah Bazile has a lifetime phobia of horses.*

I let out an uncontrollable cry. That's wrong. Totally wrong. I'm an excellent rider. I love horses. Growing up, I spent summers at the barn. My childhood bedroom had a wall full of show ribbons. I've spent thousands of hours in the saddle. This can't be right. Just like Robert's and Donna's and my parents' accusations aren't right.

"Pull yourself together," I mutter, my voice quaking. I press my hands over my ears to stop the ringing. The frustration of my writer's block, the confusion, the betrayals—it's all pressing down on me. My stress level is through the roof. I have to get a grip. Have to calm down.

CHAPTER 39

I hug my body, shoulders curled forward over my desk, trying to understand.

If my parents and Donna are telling the truth, Emma came first. I'm merely a "fragmented personality," an "alter." Is it possible this Emma person is hidden somewhere inside me, though I have no conscious awareness of her?

Is Emma aware of me? Can she sense my presence, or is she honed in on my every move? Did she see what I ate for breakfast? Did she watch me making love to Robert?

I grab my coffee, spilling it again before it reaches my lips. The absurdity of everything threatens to overwhelm me, yet I have to learn more. My need to make sense of this madness compels me to type dissociative identity disorder into my computer.

The Internet describes DID, formerly called multiple personality disorder, as two or more distinct personalities taking control of a person's behavior. The primary identity, called the "host," tends to be passive and unaware of what happens when other personalities are in control.

Donna called Emma "sweet and gentle," which could also mean passive.

According to the research, some alters are aware of the others, though they remain hidden themselves. Others have no knowledge of personalities besides their own.

Could I be an alter, only aware of myself, with no knowledge of the others? The information on my screen says some personalities exist for years without understanding what they are. But did any of them ever believe they were someone famous?

Digging deeper, I'm torn between fascination and fear, and my heart races. The mind's ability to create distinct personalities astonishes me. The human brain is wired to protect itself and survive abuse and trauma. The shift to an alter, or between alters, occurs when stressors or triggers arise. Abduction and prolonged captivity are obvious triggers.

If Emma endured captivity and abuse like Hannah, I understand why her personality split. But I don't understand how that split saved her life or got her out of there.

One arm clutching my stomach, I continue reading about DID, but it's getting harder to focus.

Incredible variances exist between alters—differences in age, gender, and even physical abilities. Some people exhibit changes in handwriting, accent, food preferences, and even allergies when a "fragmented personality" takes over. A right-handed female host and lifelong vegetarian might fragment into a left-handed male alter who speaks a different language and craves meat.

Squeezing my eyes shut, I rub my temples. I've developed a searing headache. After pushing myself out of my chair, I make it to the bathroom on shaky legs, my balance off. I pour the rest of my coffee down the drain, pop three aspirins, and guzzle a bottle of water. Moments later, I'm back on the Internet, cringing as I read. My skin is clammy, and my stomach churns with nausea, but I can't look away.

DID expert psychiatrists encourage their patients to face the trauma that caused fragmentation. It's essential to the healing process. Traumatic memories often get repressed. Writing is a powerful therapeutic tool that helps patients access and process blocked memories.

That explains why Donna and my parents would encourage me to write this book. They see it as critical therapy.

With my hands clapped over my ears, I swallow a growing lump of terror. I might be starting to believe that Hannah isn't just a character I invented. That my book isn't fiction. That I'm not who I think I am.

My fingers dig into my temples, then my scalp, trying to ward off the pain. Maybe I'm having an aneurysm, and I should call an ambulance.

Panic grips my chest, and a cold sweat trickles down my spine. I let out an inhuman, primal scream I have no control over. Something inside me is breaking free. Is this what it's like to lose your mind? Is it what I've been writing about all along?

Lightning bolts of color and sharp-angled shapes spiral and twist across my vision, then morph into a dark cloud that devours everything until I can't see at all. Wrongness invades every cell of my body.

I push against the desk to hold myself up, but it's too late. I fall forward and my head hits the hard surface.

Zipporah Bazile, the woman I thought I was, recedes into complete darkness.

PART II

KATYA

CHAPTER 40

When I lift my head from the desk, the room materializes around me like a grainy image coming into focus.

I sit up taller. Here I am. Back again.

I'm Katya Strauss. The heroine from Zipporah Bazile's *Darkness* series, but I'm more than fiction now. I'm Emma's alter.

I last surfaced at that godforsaken cabin in the wilderness. I fought my way in to save us from the sheriff. This luxury suite is no basement dungeon, that's for sure, but there's a threat. Zip isn't just pretending to be someone else—she's trying to overwrite Emma's existence. Even now, her consciousness presses against mine like a smothering hand. I press right back until the sensation subsides.

"Hello?" someone calls from outside the suite. "I'm from the front desk. Here to help with your room change."

Oh, that. "Change of plans. This room is fine. I don't need to leave anymore."

I'm here to finish our novel, but more importantly, to make sure Emma has something left of herself to return to when the manuscript is complete. I'm the type of alter who quietly watches all from the background. I saw everything Zip did here at Raven's Hollow. Let's just say I'm not her biggest fan.

Everyone wants Emma back to her old self. The sweet and optimistic woman from before the abduction. They also want to learn how she escaped her tormentor. I can give them both things. I was there. I remember every detail, the choices, and the consequences, but should I share those? I'm going to let Emma decide. The chapters I write are only for her.

I don't pretend to be a famous author, but I have Emma's best interests at heart. I'm confident I can do a decent job of reporting the truth.

I scan Zip's writing to see where she left off with Emma's story. I mean *Hannah's* story. It's obvious to me, Emma's parents, and her psychiatrists that Hannah is Emma, yet "Zipporah Bazile" didn't have a clue. She thought she was making up the entire story. She wasn't aware of much besides herself. But fine, for the sake of continuity, I'll continue calling the main character Hannah. When I'm gone and Emma comes back, she'll know who's who, and that's all that matters.

Zip also got the boyfriend's details wrong. In the real world, there was no urgent work crisis. Jackson was busy checking his car when Emma got taken. A more caring man might have walked her to the restroom instead of letting her venture into the dark alone, but Emma always settled for less than she deserved. She put everyone's needs above her own. After all of this, I hope that will change for her.

Skimming the last chapter of the manuscript, I find the protagonist where I expected "Zip" to have left her. She's trapped in that dank basement, about to shatter. It's the perfect place for me to step in.

FROM THE MANUSCRIPT

When Hannah's desperation peaks and she finally breaks, her consciousness fades into merciful oblivion in our shared mind.

While she "sleeps," I push our body off the wretched cot and into the bathroom, where I study our reflection in the hazy mirror. Hollow cheeks and sickly pale skin stare back at me. We do not look good. Not good at all. A surge of angry determination fuels me, and my fingers twitch with renewed purpose.

"My name is Katya Strauss," I say, staring our reflection square in the eye, shoulders back, chin held high. "And I'm going to get us out of here."

I'm a fragmented personality created from Emma's passion for the *Darkness* novels, but I'm the extra badass version this real-life situation requires. Emma might not have the heart for what I'm prepared to do, and that's why she's sleeping. She won't have to see any of it.

I look down at the threadbare gray socks on our feet. They're thin and pathetic, better suited for the trash, yet poor Hannah was beyond grateful to have them. That shows how far she's fallen, how thoroughly he broke her. It's the reason I'm here.

Nightmare doesn't begin to cover what's happened since her abduction, but now the terror is about to change hands.

I march back to the bedroom and hammer my fist against the door, bellowing, "Hey, you!"

The words echo off the concrete walls, and I catch myself acting stupid. Hannah would never raise her voice to him. She's been docile and compliant, clinging to the naïve hope that if she's good enough, kind enough, he'll let her go. Cooperation has not brought her freedom. Her passive strategy has left our body wasted and robbed of strength. I'll be lucky if I have the energy to climb the stairs.

Fortunately, rage brings its own kind of strength. My best chance—our best chance—lies in outwitting him, and my advantage is the element of surprise.

I knock again with less force, just loud enough to be heard, letting my voice drip with desperation. "Could you bring me some food when you have time? Thank you."

I sound just like her.

The stairs groan under the weight of his steps. It seems he keeps his boots on in the cabin, wanting to stay prepared.

The door creaks open, and there he is. Strong and handsome on the outside, hiding an ugly, sick soul.

I'm a picture of defeat huddled on the floor, skinny arms encircling stick-thin legs, eyes wide and pleading in my gaunt face. "Thank you for coming."

"Thought you'd be dead by now."

"I'm still alive. Just hungry." That's a gross understatement when I'm in the process of starving to death down here. My stomach crawls with hunger pangs sharp enough to kill. "Could you bring some food? A meat and potatoes kind of meal?" I lower my head and gaze up at him, though I'd love to tell him what he is—a psychopathic, sadistic waste of oxygen. His death would improve the world.

He jabs a finger at me. "I gave you meat. You didn't touch it."

"I've changed my mind, and I'd like some now. Please."

"Thought you were one of them vegetarians." He spits the word out with a sneer, as if it's a contagious disease.

"I was, but if I don't get more food in me, the next time you let me out to play, it won't be much of a game."

He laughs, his cruelty on display. "We're done with that. I'm finished wasting time on you."

"Wait. I'm sorry. I'll try harder. I promise I can do better. If you bring me more food, I'll show you."

I meet his gaze long enough to sell the sincerity, then curl deeper into myself, shoulders rounding, everything about my posture conveying I'm a defeated soul.

Though I may look and sound like Emma, I'm different. I'm here to save her. Things are about to change around here.

Grinning, I lean back, finished with that chapter. I'm quite proud of how it turned out.

Only when I read it over do I notice the difference between our writing. Zip wrote from a comfortable distance with her third-person, past-tense narration—*Hannah did this, Hannah did that*. I've planted myself directly into the scene and written in first person, present tense. I was there, after all. Zip wasn't. While writing *Untitled,* she could only grasp fragments of Emma's memories. Not me. Every moment of what's to come was my doing. I'll let readers crawl inside my head to see what I was thinking when I decided who deserved to live and who didn't.

CHAPTER 41

FROM THE MANUSCRIPT

When the hunter returns, he's granted my request. The plate in his hands contains hunks of raw meat swimming in crimson juices. He grins in anticipation as he awaits my reaction, expecting revulsion.

"Thank you for this feast," I say.

A grunt rumbles from his chest.

Hannah would recoil from this meal, so I tense up like it's hard for me. My grimace is real because the food is gross, but I'm ravenous. I devour every iron-rich bite, imagining strength seeping back into my bones.

"I could use seconds," I say, accidentally holding his gaze longer than she ever would. My performance isn't perfect, but it doesn't matter if I'm a little off. When he looks at me, he doesn't see me or Hannah. He doesn't see a human being. Only prey.

"You want more?" he asks with his cruel laugh. "Decided you don't want to waste away down here after all?"

I have no intention of wasting away. I'm so much stronger than he thinks. He may control what I eat, but he can't control my thoughts. Mind over matter. That's how I clawed my way to the forefront of Emma's mind. I'm here, and I need to be strong, so I am.

I accept the next serving with a "Thank you so much," layering my voice with gratitude as if he's done me an enormous favor out of the goodness of his pitch-black heart.

After he leaves, I stretch out on the cot to digest my food and gain some strength back. It doesn't take long for my feast to ignite a violent reaction in my gut. It could be due to starvation, bacteria breeding in the undercooked meat, or because Hannah's years of vegetarianism have left our body unable to handle animal protein. Whatever the reason, pain twists through my intestines like barbed wire. It won't deter me, though. I'm doubled over with nausea and cramps, but my anger burns stronger than my fever.

I can't track time in the windowless basement. Hours or an entire day go by. The space is like a large concrete coffin, and the low ceiling seems like a descending lid. A musty, decaying scent pervades everything, and the mattress reeks of sweat and past fears. How Emma survived as long as she did is beyond me. I've already had enough of experiencing this hellhole firsthand.

When he thuds down the stairs again, my spike of relief disgusts me. I'm so glad he's here, and for an instant, I forget how much I despise him. Suddenly, I can relate to Hannah's gratitude for the worthless socks and his presence. It's another reason to get out of here the minute I'm strong enough.

He carries another plate. This meal looks more edible than the last.

"You ready for more?" He shoves the plate at me.

"Yes. Thank you. I'm hungry."

He grins. Perhaps he senses a change and is excited about another round of his sick game. I want that, too. The chance to get out of this basement.

I give him a sweet smile. You stupid, arrogant man, I think. You have no idea who I am and what's coming.

As I do my best to document what unfolded in that cabin in a way that does justice to the horrors, I can still feel the hollow shell of our starved body. It was a terrible situation, but like the heroine in the *Darkness* novels, I never give up. Perseverance is a powerful weapon.

The version of me in these pages is a little dark. I'm softer in reality, though I'm fiercely protective of Emma. Now that I've emerged in two different, dire situations, I consider myself her guardian angel. I won't apologize for going a little overboard with my characterization. Stories like this one usually have larger-than-life heroes and heroines, and that's what I'm delivering. Consider it creative license. After Zip's grandiose delusions, my embellishments hardly matter.

Unlike Zip, I know my place in this hierarchy. Emma is our core. I emerge when the darkness becomes too deep for her, whether that darkness comes from outside or inside.

Zip's personality was remarkably self-centered for an alter. If she'd formed her identity around a random, unknown author, I'd find that acceptable. But no—she smugly insisted she was literary royalty, queen of the bestsellers list Zipporah Bazile.

Even when the truth stared her in the face—the pictures of the real Zipporah in Greece, the Goodreads article—she refused to believe it. More offensive was her rejection of Emma's existence. It wasn't just denial. It was an attempted coup.

Besides targeting Emma, Zip has made us look ridiculous. Or has she? Perhaps I've overestimated the damage she caused.

I replay everything about Zip's time in control. She booked the reservation and checked into Raven's Hollow using her main character's name, as if she were plotting a covert operation. Bursting with paranoia and an inflated ego, she introduced herself as Hannah to everyone she encountered around the resort. Hannah Williams isn't a real person, but using that name is better and safer than impersonating an actual celebrity. Things might not be so bad after all.

The wild card is Robert. He's the only individual outside Emma's inner circle who witnessed Zip in her full glory. But now that I'm here, I have the opportunity to change his understanding of the situation.

We haven't heard from Robert in some time. Did he give up on Zipporah that easily? He must have her pegged as a pathological liar, though every lie she told was the truth to her.

I need a break from writing. I should leave this suite and explore, find out what he's up to now.

This could be fun.

CHAPTER 42

I pull off the expensive blouse and shorts I'm wearing and leave them crumpled on the floor. In the bathroom, as I'm scrubbing Zip's make-up off my face, a sharp nail scratches my cheek. Blood-red polish on long nails isn't my style. Nor Emma's.

I rummage through the toiletry bag for nail clippers, then cut each nail down so I don't lose an eye. I'd like to get rid of the color, but our alter didn't think to pack polish remover for the trip.

Next, I tie my hair back in a low ponytail, then change into hiking pants and a navy T-shirt. When I check out my reflection in the mirror, I see no trace of Zip.

Across the hall, I rap my knuckles three times against Robert's door. I remember his last words to Zip. "If you want to talk, you know where to find me. I'm here for you." He tried so hard, and she shoved him away, convinced *he* was the unstable one. It's funny in hindsight. Poor guy. He didn't have a clue what he was walking into when he accepted that first cocktail invitation a few nights ago.

The door opens. Robert wears shorts and a polo shirt. His hand goes to his throat as if he's surprised to see me.

"Hey," I say. "I'm ready to talk."

He hesitates, and I can tell he's wary, but he steps back and opens the door wider. "Come in. Or would you rather we take a walk around the resort instead?"

"Let's grab dinner." Zip was too stressed to eat much in the past twenty-four hours, and my stomach is empty. While I'm here, unlike at the nightmare cabin, there's no reason for me to go hungry.

"Sure. Dinner works." His gaze runs over me. If he notes the difference in my appearance, he doesn't comment.

"I'm in the mood for Raven's Watch Tavern," I say because the sirloin plate Zip ordered stands out in my memory.

He nods. "Okay. Just let me put on some pants."

As he crosses the room, his muscular legs on display, I admire the view. Memories surface of him and Zip in the bedroom. He was impressive, though my frame of reference is limited to Emma's experience. I can count her sexual partners on one hand, even if she lost a few fingers.

Suddenly modest, Robert disappears into the bathroom to change.

When he emerges, he's wearing pants with the same polo shirt, rather than a dress shirt. He's deliberately dressing down to my level. Nice, right?

He clears his throat but doesn't speak. He's pieced together that "Zip" wasn't really Zip, perhaps guessed at Emma, yet he doesn't get the half of it. I've got to help him out. "I want to apologize for the confusion I've caused and make things right," I say. "Are you still interested in spending time together while we're here?"

"I am. I care about you."

That's good enough for me.

We head to the restaurant and follow the hostess to a table. Right away, we're in for an interesting surprise. Emma's parents are there. They're my parents also, in a way. Zip couldn't grasp the distinction between all of us, but it's clear to me.

I wave to reassure them I bear no hard feelings. I understand why they spied on us and encouraged Zip to write. They're simply desperate to get Emma back. Their concerns are justified.

I curl my fingers around Robert's arm. "There's some people here I want you to meet."

"Hello," they chorus, studying me. "We were worried about you."

I can practically hear their mental calculations as they try to figure out who I am. Emma? Zip? Or someone new entirely? How odd that I know everything about them, but they've never met me.

Emma, Zip, and I all look alike, though we carry ourselves differently. Most people wouldn't notice, but if anyone can pick up on our differences, it will be the people who raised Emma.

"Mom and Dad," it's odd to call them by those names, but necessary. "This is Robert Yates. My friend. I told you about him." My tone implies the drama from yesterday is behind us.

My father pushes his chair back and stands.

"And Robert, these are my parents."

Robert's eyebrows are raised. "Your parents?"

"Yes. Jack and Samantha Wilson."

I watch Robert's reaction as he registers the last name. It should reveal a lot to him.

"I didn't realize your family was here," he says.

"Until today, neither did I. It's a post-birthday surprise." I flash a smile. "And I appreciate it so much. They are the absolute best."

Robert adapts beautifully, shaking hands all around like this isn't strange at all.

"Would you like to join us?" my mother asks, despite their two-person table and nearly empty plates.

"Robert and I have some important things to discuss," I say. "But breakfast tomorrow?"

They agree with barely contained eagerness.

I place my hand on my mother's arm and lean close to her ear. "Everything is going to be fine," I whisper. "Emma will be back soon, I promise. I'll explain everything at breakfast tomorrow."

Hope glistens in her eyes. I can tell she's surprised but grateful.

At our table, Robert doesn't waste time before asking me questions. "So, your parents are here?"

"Yep. It turns out I'm seldom alone." My smile holds more secrets than he understands.

CHAPTER 43

I spend a long time studying the menu, relishing each potential choice. It's empowering to decide what to eat. Not Emma. Not Zip. Just me—Katya.

"Should we order wine?" Robert asks.

"You go ahead. I'm abstaining tonight," I say, wanting to be clear-headed and take advantage of every moment while I'm here.

"I'll pass, too," he says.

"Is your work issue settled?" I ask, setting the menu aside.

"My team has it covered."

"Good."

Our conversation might appear restrained to an observer, but it suits me fine. If Zip were still here, she'd be squirming in her seat, attempting to explain her bizarre charade and all-encompassing delusion. She deserves to be embarrassed at what she tried to pull off, though sadly, it was no act.

Jack and Samantha look my way, their concern practically radiating across the space. I smile and wave before turning my attention back to Robert. He's got to be wondering about Zip pretending to be a famous author, wondering if she's wacko or if there's another explanation. And here I am, for the most part, acting as if it never happened.

After our server recites the specials, I order two entrees and an appetizer. The bread arrives warm, and I attack it with unabashed enthusiasm.

Slathering it with butter, I take my first bite and let out an involuntary moan of pleasure. "Oh, this is so good."

"You seem different tonight," Robert says, watching me eat.

"Oh, yeah? I'm just happy to be here." I wonder if he's figured out what's going on. That's unlikely.

"I wasn't expecting you to knock on my door today, but I'm glad you did. I was supposed to leave tomorrow, but I extended my trip."

I take another piece of bread. "Oh? Why is that?"

"Because of you. I'm sorry I pushed you yesterday. I don't understand why you pretended to be someone else, but I'm sure you have your reasons." He lowers his voice. "I'm just going to lay it all out for you. I'm not leaving until I understand what's going on with us and if we have a future. I fell for you, and I thought you felt the same."

This complicates things. I didn't realize how serious he was. Zip made quite an impression. I better carefully consider my plan, but first, I just want to enjoy dinner. I cover his hand with mine. "Let's eat, and then we'll talk. How does that sound?"

"That sounds good," he says, though he must be disappointed.

When the food comes, I realize I'll never finish it all, but I try everything and enjoy it immensely.

"I noticed your parents' last name is Wilson," he says when we're finished eating. "You really are Emma?"

What should I tell him? I am, in part, Emma. We inhabit the same body, and she will return eventually. That's the main reason I'm here now, to safeguard her existence. Rather than complicate things further with directness, I can ease into the truth and fix the confusion Zip caused.

I fold my hands together, resting my chin against them. "Yes. I'm Emma Wilson. You read about my ordeal, my abduction and captivity?"

He nods, even more solemn.

"I checked in as Hannah Williams to avoid curiosity and sympathy. I'm not sure how I ended up telling you I was Zipporah Bazile. Actually, I do," I say, coming up with an idea to get us out of this problem. "It has everything to do with my book."

"So, you are a writer, then?"

"An editor, mostly, but now I'm writing."

He tilts his head and peers at me. "And you're writing a story about someone masquerading as a famous author? You just wanted to see if you could pull it off?"

I like his theory. "Well, sort of. You're the only one I told, and things got a little out of hand." I let my voice carry just the right note of embarrassment. "Do you think we could have a do-over?"

Robert keeps staring. I wish I could see what's going through his head. Finally, he says, "I saw your parents following you a few days ago. I didn't know who they were then, so it concerned me."

Ah. That explains the cryptic note Zip found in his room.

"Since I thought you were a famous author, I imagined they were members of the press who had recognized you," he continues. "I was going to mention it, but then things got a lot stranger."

That is the understatement of the year. If he weren't hooked, he would have fled this relationship by now. He must have developed genuine feelings during their twisted courtship. Or, if I'm being generous, he learned what Emma endured, and he's willing to forgive her for pretending to be someone else. Of course, that's not what happened. Zip was never pretending.

Zip's charade was bound to unravel. Eventually, Robert would find out she wasn't the famous author she claimed to be. But how did he identify her as Emma? There's one way to find out. I don't rely on assumptions or let misunderstandings escalate until they're out of control like Zip did. I believe in direct confrontation.

"How did you put together that I'm Emma? How did you find that picture of me online?"

"I did a reverse look-up with your photo. The photo of us in the café."

I rifle through memories that aren't quite mine. "Oh, the one Sarah took. Wow. I didn't even realize that was a thing, the reverse look-up."

Robert seems intelligent and open-minded. Perhaps he could handle the truth about Emma, Zip, and me. I glance around the restaurant, making sure no one is eavesdropping on our conversation. "Look, Robert, I'm not who you think I am."

Our server approaches. Terrible timing. I fall silent as he clears our plates. It's just enough of an interruption to get me second-guessing. If Robert can't handle a woman with alter personalities, he'll be out of here, and I won't have the pleasure of his company like Zip did. Besides, it's Emma's truth to tell, not mine.

When we're alone again, Robert leans toward me. "You were saying there's something I should know about you."

"Let's go for a walk. Somewhere more private."

He signals for the check, but our server tells us my parents have already handled it.

"That was generous," Robert says.

I rest my elbows on the table and say with all honesty. "They're wonderful people."

"Tell me about them."

Though we were on the verge of leaving, I settle back against my chair. "Well, they met in college. Jack is an attorney. A very successful one. And Samantha—"

"You call them Jack and Samantha?"

"Sometimes. They live in a beautiful Charlotte suburb. I've been staying with them this past year. There's plenty of room in that house. My father runs a law firm, but he's always put family first. He's always been there for us."

"And your mother? Does she work outside the home?"

"She was an oncology nurse until she stopped working to raise me. I'm their only child. They've been the best parents."

Robert's face lights up, I think in approval.

"They've supported every dream I've had, from my Olympic equestrian phase to becoming an editor. They always encouraged me to write a book. They knew how much I wanted to. When I was taken, my disappearance nearly destroyed them. They poured everything into finding me, and they'll do anything to keep me safe. That's why they followed me here."

"I can understand that," Robert says.

It's time to change focus. Other than mentioning his deceased wife, Robert shared little with Zip about his family. "Now it's your turn," I say. "Tell me about your parents and siblings, if you have any."

"I'm also lucky. My mother, Dr. Elizabeth Yates, is a pediatric psychiatrist in Seattle."

I nod, filing away the detail about his mother's profession. A psychiatrist's son may be more open to accepting unconventional truths.

Robert cups his chin. "My father, Tommy, is a mechanical engineer. They split their time between the home where I grew up in Seattle and a cabin in Montana."

"Siblings?"

"A younger brother named Matthew, and an older sister named Mia. Matthew's an architect in Seattle. Mia is a veterinarian in California with two daughters. They're six and two now."

"Are you close to your siblings?"

"Yes. We don't talk every week, but we get together often enough in Montana."

"Did you tell any of them you met Zipporah Bazile on vacation?"

Robert's smile falters. Maybe he isn't sure if we can joke about what happened, the whole pretending thing.

"I didn't mention Zipporah to anyone. You asked me to keep it private, and I did." Robert crosses his arms. "Whatever you were going to tell me, you don't have to share it if you're not ready. And if that time never comes, that's okay, too."

He thinks I was about to share details of the abduction. That's when it hits me—Robert is a good man. He keeps his word. Despite all the weirdness with Zip and the realization that, on some level, Emma must be severely traumatized, he's still here. He could have walked away, but he stayed.

"Ready to head out of here?" he asks.

We stand, and I take his hand, liking the way it feels in mine.

I guide him to my room, and once inside, I close the distance between us. "About that do-over. What do you say?" I whisper.

"I think you already know I'm all in," he murmurs, his hands finding my hips as he presses his body against mine.

With no warning, he stops and pulls his hands away, as if he's suddenly worried about hurting me. "When you were... You weren't... I mean, I don't want to..."

"If you're trying to ask me if I was sexually assaulted, the answer is no. It wasn't like that. I promise."

I can tell he's relieved for me.

Reaching for the wall switch, I kill the lights.

If this turns out to be more than a vacation romance, he might eventually learn the whole truth from Emma. But for now, while I'm in control, I plan to enjoy every moment.

CHAPTER 44

I let out a gratified sigh when I wake up. Robert and his bedroom skills did not disappoint. I'm glad I didn't scare him off.

He grins at me. "That was wild."

"It certainly was," I say, swinging my legs over the edge of the bed. "I'm tempted to lounge in bed, but I've got work to do. A novel to write."

"You're really dedicated to that story."

"Yes. My discipline is legendary." I flash him a joking smile, though the words could not be more true.

"But this will be your first novel?"

I nod. "Yep, and it's about time. I've been editing novels for almost a decade, all that time wanting to be an author."

"Will your work contacts help you get this book published?"

"Perhaps. For now, it's just for me. To prove I can do it and to help me deal with what happened."

"I see," he says.

I head to the bathroom, unconcerned with my nakedness. When I return, after stepping into shorts and a T-shirt, I go right to my desk.

Robert comes up behind me. His lips gently touch my cheek.

"I'll see you later," I say, making it a statement rather than a question. I need him to leave, but I want to see him again.

"Later, for sure. But aren't you supposed to have breakfast with your parents this morning?"

I strike the desk with my palm. I'd forgotten. It was that kind of night.

Robert steals one more kiss before letting himself out.

As I stand, I'm already thinking about what to tell Jack and Samantha. They'll want explanations and information about Emma's return.

The novel will have to wait.

Murmurs of conversation fill Raven's Watch Tavern as guests fuel up for their daily adventures. I check out the buffet, pausing to lift a few steel covers and peer inside, already planning my meal.

Jack and Samantha, impeccably dressed as usual, wait at a table set for four.

I approach with a confident smile. After all, I'm their daughter's savior, even if they don't understand that yet.

I sense their tension when I get to the table. That's not surprising, given Zip's dramatic response and rejection the other day. I intend to ease their concerns and gain their trust.

They aren't eating yet, but they have coffee. Samantha holds her mug between two hands. They're studying me, searching for clues in my movements and expressions.

Jack clears his throat and stands to greet me.

"Thank you for dinner last night," I say. "Robert and I appreciated it."

"You're welcome," he answers. "Listen, Zip, we're sorry about ambushing you in your room. It must've been quite a shock. Perhaps there was a much better way to explain."

"Better than telling the truth? Probably not. Before you go any further, I have to tell you something."

My mother is on the edge of her seat, waiting to hear what I say next.

"I'm not Zip. I'm Katya."

They exchange a quick, wide-eyed glance.

My father and I sit down.

"I'm not like Zip. I know I'm an alter." I thought that bit of information would help, but they're still confused, and I feel sorry for them. "Emma's psychiatrist was right about another alter. It's me. I got her out of that cabin. I protected her then, and I'm here to do it again."

They're spellbound now, hanging on my every word.

"Are you aware of everything that happened in the cabin? You know how Emma escaped?" Samantha asks.

I nod, keeping those dark secrets buried for now. "I can access Emma's memories, though I haven't lived them myself."

"You know everything about her? Even from when she was a little girl?" Jack asks.

"I think so." I scan my catalog of memories for moments that seem significant. "I remember an incident with you at Lake Tahoe. You were visiting your brother's family. Emma was around five, and you took her fishing. She screamed her head off when you pulled the fish out of the water and ripped the hook out. After that, she couldn't look at you for days."

Jack's thick eyebrows rise. "You wailed like a banshee and wouldn't stop. People thought I was hurting you. You made a huge scene."

"It wasn't me. It was Emma. She thinks fishing for sport is cruel."

Samantha nods. "She does. She does."

What else can I share? "Oh, one of her favorite memories is winning the champion division at a horse show in New York. She was riding a horse named D.J. No one expected that horse to place."

Samantha and Jack break into affectionate smiles. "You loved that horse," Samantha murmurs.

"Emma loved that horse," I say.

They have more questions, but I stop them for now. "The buffet is incredible. Can we talk over food?"

Assembling my breakfast, I shovel bacon and sausage on my plate, along with eggs, a biscuit, melon, and oatmeal with nuts and berries. I want it all. Emma is a vegetarian, but these animals already died, and I don't think I'll be around long enough to damage any arteries with my diet. Besides, if Emma's return is anything like last time, she won't recall what I ate while she was gone. Unless her parents tell her, she won't even realize I was here, except for the manuscript I'll leave behind.

I'm enjoying my breakfast when Samantha says, "I'm still confused about how all of this works, but you've convinced me you're not Emma, and you're not Zipporah."

I nod because my mouth is full.

Samantha continues, "Are you also aware of everything that happened when Zipporah was the personality in charge?"

A laugh escapes me at Zip's name, and I cover my mouth with my hand until I've swallowed my food. "Yes. That was quite the performance, wasn't it?"

The lighthearted moment dies as darker thoughts surface. Right from the start, Zip's intentions troubled me. She intended to kill the book's main character because she was weak. Maybe Zip didn't fully understand what she was doing, but on some level, she wanted to write Emma out of existence.

That's not going to happen now. With me in charge, *Untitled* will get the ending it deserves. Not a happy ending, but a healing one. The main character will live. The truth will bring Emma back. That's the reason I'm here, my true purpose, though I'm currently stuffing my face with the buffet.

"Do you think Emma will remember you?" Samantha asks.

"I can't say. You'll have to ask her when she returns."

Hope flickers across their faces at the mention of Emma's return. They're putting up with me, but I'm not their first choice.

"I'm here to work on the novel. I'll write about the parts that happened when I was the dominant. It won't be easy for Emma to read the manuscript when I'm gone, but she needs to know so she can move on."

"That sounds wonderful, Katya." Samantha says my name as if we're playing a child's pretend game. That's fine with me. Whatever works for them. I get that this is a very peculiar situation.

Jack clasps his hands together. "We're right here, just a phone call away if you need us for anything at all. Like you, we plan to check out on Wednesday. We have a rental car."

"Great. Keep me updated on when we're leaving. I'm going back with you. To your house. It's the only place I've got."

"Of course," Jack answers. "We're happy to have you with us for as much time as you need, Katya."

His words are kind, but I see the truth he's hiding. They'll tolerate me because they have to. I'm in their daughter's body. But they're desperate for me to disappear and give them Emma back.

I understand, but I have work to finish first. And just a little more fun while I'm here.

CHAPTER 45

B reakfast with Jack and Samantha went well, and I'm back in my suite, armed with black coffee and focused. I'm completely embracing this writing challenge. I'm eager to reveal the truth that's been a secret for so long. It's all for Emma. I hope it's what she needs.

I won't shield her or coddle her. She can form her own opinions and draw her own conclusions.

FROM THE MANUSCRIPT

Heavy footsteps clomp down the basement stairs and across the cement floor. The lock turns, and he enters. I've been perfecting my vulnerable look in the bathroom mirror. My sallow complexion helps. I use the practiced expression now, keeping my head lowered and averting my eyes as he places an oval platter on the floor. The smell of food triggers a rumble in my stomach.

"Thank you. How lucky I am to have a host who can cook."

Perhaps I'm overselling it, but there's a delicious irony in pretending to be so docile while plotting to put an end to a monster.

"I don't cook. It's grilled. Have at it." He sneers as he locks the door behind him, leaving me alone again.

The platter holds a large, lumpy serving of unrecognizable meat. It's far from a choice cut of anything, with bones and gristle scattered throughout. Nothing resembling this exists in the meat section of the grocery store, yet it's exactly what I need.

I tear into it with my hands, stripping slimy flesh from the bones while grimacing at the taste and texture. The largest piece I set aside. It's for Bolton. He and I need to become friends.

As I eat, I consider options to win the guard dog's affection, so it won't attack me. I don't want to hurt him. If Hannah found out, she'd never forgive me. I can imagine her saying "It's not his fault. He's innocent and as trapped as I am."

It's fascinating that Hannah isn't aware of my presence or what I'm doing. She's blissfully unaware of our current situation. While I devise our escape, she sleeps in the dark, the same way she did before birth.

Finished eating, I remove the bone fragments from the remains of my mystery meat and tuck them into a pocket of my tattered clothing. The largest bone—a second gift for Bolton—goes into the back pocket of my jeans.

I'm washing meat juice off my hands at the bathroom sink when the hunter returns for his platter.

"Finally got some sense in you," he grunts, apparently pleased, or amused, that I've eaten his sickening meal.

"Thank you," I tell him through gritted teeth.

After he leaves, I'm left waiting in the small room that reeks of decay. Even after showering, I still smell unwashed, which I can't explain unless I am rotting and decomposing from the inside out, which is possible.

The food settles in my stomach, and my insides remain calm. As I lie on the cot, my fingers trace the bones in my pocket, and my mind spins with thoughts of retribution. With nothing else to do down here, it's become an obsession.

The timing needs to be right, although it may never be perfect. I have to make sure he doesn't suspect a thing until it's too late.

When enough hours have passed, I crouch at the door with the first bone fragment. Peering into the lock mechanism, I attempt to slide the bone into the tiny opening. It's too large, so I choose another and start again, careful not to make any noise. Hannah was always quiet, except for the time she heard voices upstairs.

The second bone slides in, and I move it up and down. The lock resists, so I press harder. With a quick snap that makes me wince, the bone breaks into three pieces and becomes useless.

I stand and force myself to calm down, to steady my hands. There's only one thin bone left.

This one glides into the lock as though it were waiting for this moment. With less force this time, I press it against the spring-loaded pins, listening for a click.

Nothing happens. My fingers cramp, and my legs shake from crouching. I withdraw my makeshift tool and shuffle around the room for a bit, rubbing my neck. Failure is not an option.

When I'm crouched down and hunched over again, chewing on my chapped bottom lip, I hear it. An almost imperceptible click.

I turn the knob and pull the door open. Seconds later, I'm walking through. Quietly, I close the door behind me and engage the exterior lock.

With adrenaline heightening my senses, I take quiet, cautious steps up the basement stairs. I pause in the dark cabin, listening for the slightest hint of movement and preparing my next moves.

I am the plot twist my captor didn't see coming.

As I put the final touches on that chapter, an icy dread settles over me. I'm remembering what I did next.

I have to stop writing for a while. My legs are tingling from sitting so long in one position. The rest of the story will have to wait.

I text Robert. *Want to go mountain biking?*

His response comes quickly. *Meet you at the equipment building in an hour.*

Perfect. Creating new memories helps escape the dark ones.

CHAPTER 46

Pure freedom is flying down the hill on a mountain bike. The wind whips my hair back, and there's a huge grin plastered across my face. Sprays of crystal-clear water shoot up around us as I follow Robert across the creek at the bottom. On the other side, I stand and pump my legs hard, maneuvering around rocks and roots.

The resort's well-maintained forest trails bear no resemblance to that other forest with its twisted brambles and hidden traps. Here, the obstacles make me cry out with laughter.

My legs burn, and my heart pounds, but this isn't a desperate race for survival. I'm alive and breathless in an extraordinary, exhilarating way.

The sun is low in the afternoon sky when we stop on a hill and admire the view. A beautiful lake shimmers below us.

Straddling my bike, I move closer to Robert. "Mind if we take a selfie?"

He takes my phone, extending his arm to frame us with the forest as the backdrop. "Smile," he says, and I do. He takes another photo with my head against his shoulder, and we stay that way, leaning into each other and enjoying the moment. Something inside me aches when we finally move to leave. I don't want this ride, this day, or this trip to end. I wish I could stay at Raven's Hollow.

Back at the resort, I remove my helmet and dab perspiration from my forehead with the back of my hand, already thinking about what we can do next. "I could go for an iced tea and some food."

"Sounds good to me," Robert says as I adjust my ponytail. "You always wore your hair down before. Now it's always up."

"Oh? Keeping track of my hairstyles, are we? I like that you noticed."

"I notice a lot about you," he says, his fingers tracing my jaw and lingering on my throat.

In leather chairs by the café's front window, we order drinks and a shared plate of cheese, crackers, and fruit. I don't have to inspect my food or worry about finding crushed meds in my drink. Gone is the need for anti-depressants and other pills. I'm in control now. I've got this.

Sitting across from each other, Robert and I relive the most exciting moments from our bike ride: the jump that sent me airborne and made me scream, the fast turn where he wiped out but luckily wasn't hurt.

During a lull in our conversation, I gaze out the café's window. I'm having such a good time that I've almost forgotten my purpose here. I should work on the novel. But there's no pressing urgency. No one is starving and nearing death while locked in a basement. Emma is fine for now.

"Everything okay?" Robert asks, pulling me back to the present.

In response, I get up and slide into his chair with him, weaving my ankles between his. There's danger in this simple, intimate act. It's not the same sort of danger as being chased through the woods by a cruel hunter. The comfort I'm feeling with Robert has the potential to hurt me in a different way.

Robert is a good person. I'm more convinced of that with each passing hour. But there's more I must uncover about him.

"Do you mind talking about your wife?" I ask, my question likely surprising him.

His mouth closes, his lips forming a thin line, but he doesn't look away. "Anything specific?"

"What was her name?"

"Danielle. And to be honest, I've been thinking about her a lot today."

That's a strange thing to say, and now I'm the surprised one. "More than usual?"

"I have, since yesterday. You and she would have liked each other. You share the same passion for life."

"Was it a good marriage?" I ask, though from his tone when he talks about her, the answer seems obvious.

Robert takes my hand in both of his. "Yes. It ended too soon. We didn't have enough time. While we were married, we were both devoted to our careers. I was building my business and traveling a lot. I loved Danielle, but I only truly realized how lucky we were once she was gone." His voice cracks. "As I told you before, I learned the hard way that we can't predict how much time we have in life or with each other. We have to make the most of every day."

"I'm sorry, Robert." I'm distracted by what he said, the part about predicting our time. I'm the exception. My time will end once I complete the novel. I'll leave so Emma can reclaim her life.

A lump forms in my throat, surprising me. This thing with Robert is real in a way I never expected.

"After we leave here, when can I see you again?" he asks.

I swallow hard. I can't maintain eye contact with him. "After I finish my first draft."

"What if I flew you to Seattle, and you could write in my home office? It's not Raven's Hollow, but the view is nice. I can promise to leave you alone during the day so you can focus on your book if that's what you need. I don't mean to pressure you. Just think about it, okay?"

"I will."

Once I'm in the privacy of my room, I get on the Internet. Given my connection to Robert, I need to understand him better.

Robert sounded sincere when talking about his late wife. But what if her death wasn't an accident? That's how my brain works. I expect the worst of people. It's a direct result of my experience in that secluded cabin. The ordeal taught me to trust no one.

My goal is to make sure Robert is innocent of his wife's death, yet I'm mentally prepared to find the opposite.

My search starts with: Danielle Yates + obituary + Seattle.

Obituary for Danielle Yates

Seattle, Washington - Danielle Stewart Yates, beloved wife, cherished daughter, and dedicated environmentalist, passed away tragically on August 13, surrounded by her family.

Danielle was born in Tacoma, Washington, to Barry and Lola Stewart. From an early age, she loved nature and had a deep respect for the environment.

Danielle pursued a graduate degree in environmental science from the University of Washington. Her dedication to environmental causes drew her to the nonprofit company Eco Vision. For the last seven years, she championed the preservation of wilderness areas.

Danielle's passions included hiking, kayaking, and rock climbing.

Tragically, her life got cut short while climbing with two friends at Tieton River Canyon in Washington when an accident occurred. Despite the immediate response of rescue teams and the excellent efforts of medical professionals, Danielle succumbed to her injuries. Her husband Robert was out of the country but returned in time to be by Danielle's side in her final moments.

I skim back to the top of the article and fixate on the date of her death. August 13th. Today is August 22nd, and Robert has been at Raven's Hollow for over ten days.

His visit coincides with the anniversary of his wife's death. That seems significant. Whether he's here to honor her memory or escape his grief, one important fact stands out. Robert wasn't with Danielle when she had her accident. He isn't responsible for her death, and he's just cleared one more hurdle.

CHAPTER 47

My time at Raven's Hollow is slipping away. Less than twenty-four hours remain before my scheduled checkout time. There are a hundred things I'd rather do at the resort, but my sense of responsibility keeps me at my desk. I'm determined to complete one more chapter before I leave.

The previous chapter concluded with my escape from the basement room, placing me inside the cabin. This is where my story truly begins.

FROM THE MANUSCRIPT

I hesitate at the top of the basement stairs. It's dark inside the cabin. Bolton will either hear me or pick up my scent first. I've got a hunk of meat and the bone I saved for him. I'm betting everything on his appetite being stronger than his instinct to guard. When I don't see or hear the dog, I begin to move about.

My vision adjusts to the shadows. Pieces of furniture take shape before me.

A quick scan of counters and drawers reveals no keys. Not that I expected it to be that easy. The hunter's truck is gone, and his dog and his only set of keys must be with him. I suppress the instinct to flee the cabin and race into the woods while I can. But that's not enough. I'm here to end this.

First, I need fuel.

I turn on a light in the kitchen and check the refrigerator. Ceramic jugs crowd the top shelf. I open one, and the sharp odor burns my nostrils. Moonshine is the sheriff's drink of choice.

The cabinets are more promising. I tear into a sleeve of some generic brand crackers and shove a handful in my mouth. Plain crackers have never tasted so good. I grab a jar of peanut butter, then search for a spoon. Inside the utensil drawer is a knife sharp enough to do some real damage.

With a mouthful of peanut butter, I head for the stack of mail on the counter. The envelopes are addressed to *Travis Cockeram, 2401 Mountain Gap Trail, Lenoir, NC.*

Finally, I've learned his name. "Well, Sheriff Travis," I whisper, "let's see what else you're hiding here."

The peanut butter returns to the shelf, and I hide the dirty spoon in the garbage.

It's time to go exploring.

I'm drawn to a door off the kitchen that turns out to be a storage space. Two freezer chests dominate the small room. I imagine their contents—frozen bodies, frosted lashes staring up from unseeing eyes. I'm too late to save them, but I must learn what Travis is capable of doing.

Bracing myself to view the dead body of another victim, I grasp the handle of the first freezer and pull the heavy top open. I'm not surprised to see a giant slab of frozen meat, but the ribcage is too large to be human. The second freezer contains the same.

A plain metal box sits in one corner, but a padlock prevents me from looking inside. It probably contains a cache of rifles and ammunition. If only he'd left a rifle out for me like he did with Hannah. I've never fired one either, but I'm willing to learn.

The cabin remains silent as I head down the main floor's hallway and peek into the rooms. Everything in the main bathroom is clean and neat. The countertop holds a toothbrush, toothpaste, a straight razor, and shaving cream.

My interest lies inside the medicine cabinet. The shelves have an arsenal of sleep aids. I'm familiar with the labels and compounds. Emma's grandmother owns a similar collection. The drugs tell me Travis has serious sleep issues, though I can't fathom what keeps him up at night, considering he has no conscience.

I gather the liquid formulations and carry them into the kitchen. There, I dump most of the sedatives into a ceramic jar at the fridge's front and give it a good stir. This concoction should, at a minimum, knock him off his game.

Travis isn't my only threat. There's also his dog. After finding the animal's bowls, I doctor the water with sedatives and soak the meat I'm gifting him into the mixture. I keep the bone. I might need it for what comes next.

Everything goes back where I found it, and I continue my search.

The sheriff wasn't expecting me to ascend from his dungeon and rummage through his things today, so he didn't lock his closets or doors. I select a heavy camouflage coat, gloves, hat, and a sweater to keep me warm outside until he returns. The knife I took fits inside the coat's deep pockets.

A wooden box on the top shelf of his closet is the right size for a handgun. I stand on a stool to pull the box down. It's not locked. When I open it, I'm disappointed there's no gun. It only holds newspaper clippings.

A black-and-white photograph of Hannah stares up at me from the top clipping. The caption reads: *Woman Goes Missing in NC. Local Sheriff Vows to Find Her.*

Fury boils inside me as I read how Travis promised to find the woman he's holding captive.

Hannah Williams disappeared from a rest area off Highway 77 on the evening of December 7th. Hannah is five foot six and weighs approximately one hundred and twenty pounds. She has brown hair and brown eyes. She was last seen wearing jeans and a black winter coat.

Hannah's parents are offering a $100,000 reward to anyone with information on her whereabouts. Three million dollars to anyone who can guarantee her safe return.

I put aside the article about Hannah to see what else the box contains. The next clipping from two years ago makes me gasp.

Maggie Lewis, missing. Last seen in Lenoir, NC.

Beneath the article about Maggie, there's one more, from four years back. The thin paper is yellowed and ripped along one edge.

Kimberly Jones vanished without a trace.

The article about Kimberly includes an image of Travis Cockeram. He's behind a podium, wearing his sheriff's uniform, again promising to find her.

The tally marks on the basement wall have names now. Maggie Lewis and Kimberly Jones. The extent of the sheriff's evil makes my nostrils flare. He abducts women and pretends to search for them.

The clippings join the knife in my pocket. My desire to make Travis pay has reached a new level. There will not be any more missing women in this cabin.

Bundled under layers of clothing that reeks of moonshine—it probably sweats out of his pores—I'm almost ready to head out.

Atop the fireplace mantle are a flashlight and a whistle. I take both.

Last, I discover the night-vision goggles hanging by the door.

"Thank you. Don't mind if I do," I whisper through clenched teeth as I add those to my collection of supplies.

Sheriff Travis is in for a real surprise.

<hr>

Weary but satisfied, I close the laptop for the night and tune in to my surroundings. Night fell while I was writing. Through the balcony windows, glowing lights dot the resort, shimmering like fireflies, but beyond the property's edge, the mountain woods are a vast stretch of blackness.

My chair scrapes the floor as I push away from the desk and appreciate the room, wishing Emma could see it. The resort selected everything for its beauty and comfort: the luxurious designer bedding, a selection of coffees and teas, and the original artwork on the walls. It's the exact opposite of Travis's basement prison.

After reliving those moments in the cabin and thinking about Travis, I'm desperate to see Robert again. I want a reminder that genuine goodness exists in men.

CHAPTER 48

On the balcony of the main lodge, the mountain air is crisp enough to warrant a sweater. Robert and I stand side by side, hips touching, taking turns studying the stars through the telescope. While I gaze outward, the gentle weight of his hand rests against my lower back. We trade places, and my fingers trace a path over his shoulders. Touching him feels so right and natural, yet I'll soon have to give it up.

Robert moves from the telescope. His face breaks into an unguarded smile.

I raise my phone. "Hold on. Don't move." I seize the moment in a snapshot, then nestle against him for a selfie. I want evidence we existed here, together.

We're both aware tomorrow morning marks the end of our stay, and our last few hours are precious. Uncovering Emma's history has heightened Robert's concern and caring. He's protective, as if he thinks I could suddenly vanish. That isn't too far from the truth.

"I have something for you," he whispers, drawing me closer. "Come to my room with me."

In his suite, he presents me with a small, wrapped box. Inside the box is a silver necklace with a raven pendant. It's a charming souvenir from the resort's gift shop. I love it.

His fingers trail across my neck as he fastens the clasp.

"Send me the photos you took," he says ."I'm going to look at them every day until we see each other again."

I send them to his phone, and he studies each one like he's memorizing the details.

A now familiar ache builds in my chest. This thing between us is special. When I go and Emma returns, will she remember anything of these moments?

Robert is nothing like Emma's former boyfriend. Jackson couldn't handle her abduction. He couldn't bear the weight of her trauma and his guilt. Their relationship ended soon after Emma's return. Jackson cut loose when she needed him most. He wasn't the right guy for her, but Robert's commitment is a promising sign. He's like me. Not a quitter.

Emma needs someone like him in her life, a good man willing to stand by her side despite her trauma and the uncertainties that lie ahead. She needs someone brave enough to face the darkness with her when I'm not here.

Seattle and Charlotte are opposite sides of the country, but long-distance relationships can work and there's no good reason Emma can't move if she wants to.

I can envision Emma and Robert building a real future together and finding lasting happiness. I'm no psychiatrist, but I believe the bond I'm building with Robert will be just as important for Emma's healing as understanding what happened at that cabin.

Perhaps, someday, she can tell him everything.

After my alarm goes off, Robert and I linger in my bed until the last possible moment, until we have no choice but to disentangle our bodies. I barely have enough time to shower and pack.

When I exit my suite with my suitcases in tow, he's waiting in the corridor with a luggage cart.

Our walk to the main lodge is a bittersweet journey. With each step, my heart grows heavier. The intensity surprises me. I'm almost weepy and ill about leaving him. Yet, I'm also glad it's happening now. The longer I stay at this resort, a world more mine than Emma's, the more devastating it becomes to say goodbye.

Samantha is waiting on the lodge steps in casual pants and a cotton T-shirt. Her shoulder-length hair is pulled back.

"You look so much like your mother," Robert says.

"I do, don't I?" Even that sentiment fills me with melancholy.

I'm sure Samantha and Jack are curious about Robert and me. They must have questions about what will happen next. I have those same questions, though I have a plan. When I finish the novel and I'm gone, I want Emma and Robert to find love together. Facilitating that is part of my commitment to help her.

"Good morning, Robert," Samantha says.

"Good morning. Tough to leave this place, isn't it?"

"Yes, the resort was wonderful, but no matter where we go, I like getting home and back to my regular life." She turns to me. "How are you today?" She makes a move to touch me but withdraws her hand. Instead, she studies me, perhaps searching for signs that I'm still Katya.

"I'm fine. Still here. Same as yesterday. And you?"

"I'm well. Your father went to get the car. Oh, here he is now."

An SUV pulls up near us. Jack sits behind the wheel.

Samantha heads to the car, leaving Robert and me alone. It's time for a last goodbye.

"As soon as I finish my novel, I'll call you. Okay?" It's all I can do to get the words out.

"As in, don't call me. I'll call you?" The hurt in his eyes makes me want to explain everything.

"It won't take me too long. I'll talk to you soon. I promise." Another necessary lie.

Robert nods. "Have a safe trip back. And finish your draft asap because I'm going to miss you."

"Same," I manage. "It shouldn't be more than a few days. I just need to focus."

After a final embrace, a last moment of direct physical contact for me, I let go of him and walk backwards, waving as I go, to join Jack and Samantha.

"That was an interesting trip," Samantha says as we pull away, leaving Raven's Hollow behind us.

With a heavy, dull ache in my chest, I turn, watching the resort growing smaller in the distance until we round a bend, and I can no longer see it.

We're quiet for a while as Jack navigates the twisty mountain roads. He catches my eye in the rearview mirror. "I had the firm's private investigator check into Robert. No red flags with him. He's a respected business person running a cyber security company. He was married once, but his wife passed away. A very tragic story."

"I know," I cut in. "I spent a lot of time with him, and so did Zip. He's a good man. Kind and caring."

Jack clears his throat, his eyes on the road. "Who does he think you are?"

"He thinks I'm Emma and that I pretended to be someone else when we first met, for the sake of my novel."

"What does he know about Emma?" Samantha asks.

"He read about her abduction. He discovered the information online. Those were the notes Zip found in his room. But that's all he knows about what happened. He never pushed for details about the captivity or the escape."

We're quiet again until I add, "He's planning on seeing me again. He invited me to Seattle."

Samantha lets out a surprised, "Oh. Are you going?"

"No, though I'd like to. I want Emma to meet him when she comes back. He's the kind of man she deserves. She'll have to give him a chance and learn to trust him. That will be the hard part."

Despite all my good intentions and an excellent grasp of my role here, it's hard for me to talk about handing Robert over to someone else. Even if that person is Emma.

"This is all very difficult to swallow," Samantha says, turning around in her seat to face me in the back. "We're talking about Emma in the third person, as if she's somewhere else."

"She is," I say. "She's sleeping."

"You're in her body, and you look like her, yet you're so different."

"Yes, in some ways. But I'm part of her. I'm what she needs." As I say that, I realize it might be the same with Zip. Maybe Emma needed the unabashed confidence Zip brought to writing the novel. She got Emma started.

"Now what? What happens next?" Jack asks.

"I only have a few more chapters to write. Once I finish, I'll be on my way."

Samantha twists strands of her hair between her fingers. "You'll just leave and let Emma take your place? Is that how it works?"

"I'll make sure that's what will happen."

She extends her arm between the seats and takes my hand. "Thank you," she whispers.

When she lets go of my hand, I turn to the window and fix my gaze on the passing scenery. Tears threaten to fall, but I blink them back, my fingers clutching the raven pendant at my neck. I'm here to provide strength and protect Emma. I can't show weakness, and I won't. Though I'm starting to worry about myself as much as her.

CHAPTER 49

I follow Jack and Samantha through the double front doors of their home. Emma has lived with them since she escaped the hunter's cabin. They've done all they could to help her heal.

Jack rolls our suitcases inside then turns to me, as if we've come this far and now he's unsure what to do next.

"Home at last," I say, since I can tell he's at a loss for words.

He smiles, then covers a yawn with his hand. "I'm beat. Goodnight." He dips his head at me before heading straight for his bedroom.

"I'm going to unpack and head to bed." Samantha seems hesitant to leave me alone.

"Go ahead. I know where everything is. Don't worry about me."

"Good night, then." She hugs me before walking away.

The long flight east and late dinner inside the Charlotte airport left us drained, but I followed my meal with a large black coffee. I'm wired.

I move through rooms the housekeepers have prepared for our return. Everything looks and smells familiar, a mixture of the freshly baked bread they left for us, and a hint of citrus from cleaning solutions. I stroll through the breakfast nook and into the family room. Every detail I take in is sharper and more vivid than I've experienced it before. It's like getting a stronger eyeglass prescription and noticing the little things you previously couldn't.

The framed photos on the walls showcase Emma's life—family vacations, college graduation, equestrian events, birthdays. The images capture her smiling face from the days before Sheriff Travis Cockeram took her. A family portrait hangs over the mantle. It's another snapshot of happier times before Emma's abduction, when this family was still whole.

I carry my things upstairs to Emma's bedroom, which is immaculate and orderly thanks to the housekeepers. I unpack and return the *Darkness* novels to a bookshelf displaying hardcover copies of every book Zipporah Bazile has ever written. Several of the novels contain the author's signatures.

Neat piles of journals, sticky notes, and colored pens grace Emma's desk, though it's been over a year since she did any writing or editing. She's on leave from the publishing company. They're holding a position for her, which doesn't surprise me. She was an excellent editor and did far more work than they paid her for.

In Emma's house, surrounded by her belongings, I'm acutely aware of why I'm here.

I can't let the abduction haunt her forever. She has to move on.

A few minutes later, I'm seated at Emma's desk, typing away.

FROM THE MANUSCRIPT

Outside the nightmare cabin, bundled under layers of the sheriff's clothing, I fumble with the night vision goggles. I can't get them to work.

There's no obvious switch or button. It doesn't matter. Even if I can't turn them on, if I have them and he doesn't, that's enough. I hurl them deep into the brush where they're unlikely to get found. I've got his flashlight, and that will have to do. Sliding my fingers into his thick gloves, I head down the dirt road. On my way, I spot a fallen branch about three feet long and pick it up. I'm going to need it.

After a few minutes of walking on the road, I push into the woods through a tangle of brush and sharp branches that scrape against my stolen coat. Wary of concealed traps, I aim the flashlight down and probe with my stick as if it's a blind person's cane. I half-expect to hear the ominous click of a landmine or metal snapping shut around my ankle and yanking me up into the trees. My fear sharpens my senses. It might be the thing that will keep me alive as I navigate Travis's killing grounds.

My movements have become a slow ritual—shine the flashlight into the inky darkness, test the ground with my stick, take a few steps, and repeat. It goes on like that for a long time until my stick plunges through empty air and momentum pitches me forward. Arms flailing, I grab a branch just in time to keep from falling. When my heart stops thundering against my ribs, I shine the flashlight and peer down into a gaping hole.

He's hidden this trap well. It had looked like a solid section of the forest floor, but it's not. Sharp wooden spears protrude upward from a deep pit like a medieval torture chamber. I pity whatever innocent creature stumbles in.

The rumble of an engine resonates through the woods. When I see the vehicle's headlights through the trees, I kill my light and sink into the underbrush, around fifteen yards from where Travis's truck passes.

He's back. This is the hard part. I have to wait. He needs time to guzzle his doctored moonshine, but not so much time that I risk hypothermia in the frigid night air. Not so much that he goes into the basement and discovers I'm gone. The latter is unlikely, as he rarely bothers to check on me.

My muscles protest the cold as I pace the area, retracing the route from the road to the pit, memorizing every tree. When I face Travis, I need to be as comfortable with this small area of the woods as he is. My plan unfurls in my mind, and I rehearse the possibilities.

The cold burrows deeper into my bones. Months of starvation are taking their toll. I can't stay on my feet much longer. It's time. It has to be.

My gloved fingers fumble in my pocket, and I retrieve the whistle. I purse my lips and blow. A haunting, high-pitched wail echoes through the quiet forest. After a few seconds, I blow again.

The device mimics an animal's call. Maybe a deer or a bobcat. Any animal will do, as long as it lures Travis here. Either because he thinks there's another hunter on his property or something out here for him to kill.

I wait, shivering violently now, teeth clattering, then send another call into the night. My legs cramp, and my face burns with cold, but none of that matters.

It doesn't take long to hear a rustling sound. Someone or something large is moving through the forest. It must be him.

Every nerve in my body ignites. I blow the whistle one last time. Gripping the hunting knife, I try not to move a muscle and clamp my teeth together to stop the chattering.

When I peek through the leaves, a small circle of light moves in my direction. The beam comes toward me, cutting small arcs through the darkness. I don't hear the dog. If my plan worked, Bolton found the meat, drank his water, and now sleeps peacefully back at the cabin.

My heart is practically exploding in my chest. For one terrible moment, doubt crashes over me. This could go catastrophically wrong. Travis is a real hunter with an arsenal of weapons. If he shoots in my direction, I'm done. I've failed.

But he thinks Hannah is locked in the basement, and he probably drank the sedative-laced moonshine. I'm counting on those drugs to reduce his enormous advantages.

Travis steps into view with a raised rifle. Bolton isn't with him.

Biting my lip to stifle any sound, I wait for the perfect moment. He's close, but not close enough.

His head swivels, and suddenly, we're locked in a stare that stops my heart. I don't breathe. I count to five before his gaze slides past. He didn't see me.

I explode from my hiding place and slam into him. The collision sends him stumbling. His rifle thwacks the ground, and I'm on his back instantly, driving the knife into the side of his neck. In my ideal scenario, I slit his neck from side to side. But that's not what happens. Cords of thick muscle block my thrust. I've hurt him, but he's still alive.

His howl rips through the night as his elbow drives back. The blow slams into my right eye and sends me sprawling.

He leaps up, hands clutching his throat.

This is the moment that matters. I retreat toward the pit, letting him see me cower.

"I'm going to kill you," he gurgles, blood bubbling with each word.

He moves toward me.

The pit lies mere inches from my right foot. Just one more step. That's all it will take, just one more.

"You aren't as clever as you think, Travis." I taunt him despite my terror. I need him blinded by fury.

"Stop talking, little Hannah," he says through wet, raspy breaths. "I want to hear you scream when I kill you."

"I'm not Hannah," I spit back, though I'm shaking. "You've got the wrong woman. Hannah's gone. I'm what's left after you broke her."

When he lunges for me, his boot skids out from under him, and his arms fly upward.

I kick him with everything I have, and it's enough to send him plunging downward.

Bone-snapping cracks and wretched screams fill the night.

On my knees at the pit's edge, I stare down at Travis. When his screams die, I use his flashlight to illuminate his broken, twisted body.

A phone rings from below, startling me. Travis doesn't move. Only his rapidly blinking eyes tell me he's still alive.

I glare down at him with my hands on my hips. "You going to get that? Do you want to tell them the sheriff needs help? Though I don't think you'll last long enough. You don't look so good."

He doesn't answer, but I think he registers that I stole his evil words and made them the last he'll hear.

"You made it too easy," I say, mocking him. "Sleep tight, Travis."

The chapter I just wrote disturbs me, but it's the truth. A session with Donna might offer insights into my behavior, although I already understand my motives. My actions stemmed from watching Hannah's helplessness from the sidelines. My goal was to get her out of that basement and that wilderness alive, but I couldn't stop there. I had to get justice for Emma and the other captives—Maggie Lewis and Kimberly Jones.

Travis Cockeram pushed Emma until she broke. He died in a brutal trap of his design. He got what he deserved, and I have no regrets. I did it for Emma.

CHAPTER 50

I spend my first day at "home" exploring the Wilson's estate and relaxing, rather than writing. I roam the gardens, and I'm mesmerized by bees collecting pollen from plump flower blossoms and squirrels visiting the bird feeders. Like Emma in her younger days, I swim laps in the pool, then nap on a lounge chair with the sun warming my skin. Later, I replace the chipped red polish on my nails with a clear coat.

Samantha offers me food throughout the day, but I prefer to get my own. I raid the pantry and the fridge for each meal, trying new things and eating until I'm stuffed.

When evening arrives, I sit by the pool again with an iced tea and a board of cheese and crackers I've prepared, thinking about what else I should tell Emma before I go. It's quiet and peaceful in the private yard. Shadows stretch from the tall bushes and reach the water as the landscape lighting comes on. I wish Robert were here to enjoy it with me.

It's a shame Emma has spent little time outside lately. She can and should enjoy this life whenever she wants.

I'm on my way inside when Samantha comes to say goodnight. "Can I get you anything before I head to bed?" she asks.

I glance at the crumbs on my board and the empty iced tea bottle I'm carrying and smile. "No, thanks. I'm good."

"Will you be up much longer?"

She and Jack must wonder how much I have left to write, but they're too kind to push. It would be like asking a house guest what time they plan on leaving. I appreciate their tact. They're part of the reason Emma exudes kindness and compassion. If they ever read about how I dealt with the sheriff, their opinions of me might change. I have to remind myself that regardless of my methods, I saved us. That's what matters. I saved their daughter. I'm the reason Emma can come back.

"I'm going to write a bit more before calling it a night." I set the cutting board down and embrace Samantha. I'm following Robert's advice to cherish every precious moment.

Samantha hugs me back. When we let go of each other, she says, "Good night. Sleep tight."

A wave of revulsion hits me at those words. It's not her fault. She doesn't understand how many times Travis repeated that phrase to Emma in his mocking, callous tone. She can't know those were the last words *he* ever heard. In my mind, they'll forever be associated with Travis, yet those aren't the only reasons the phrase spooks me now. I'm putting up a brave front, but the idea of leaving, of going to "sleep," depresses me more than I'd like to admit. It's because of what I'm giving up. My current situation isn't like being captive in that cabin, slogging through the woods in a malnourished, weak body, fighting to survive in freezing temperatures. This place and these people are great. I'm comfortable and safe. Letting go won't be easy.

I'm mentally and physically healthy and strong, so barring an unexpected event, my transition will require a conscious and focused effort on my part. I'll have to relinquish control and allow Emma to return.

All is quiet in the house after Samantha retreats to her bedroom and closes the door.

I walk through the French doors at the side of the house and onto the porch, where I lean against the iron railing. The night sky is cloudless, the stars bright. I grasp the raven pendant around my neck. I'm tempted to call Robert, but I won't. I want so badly to accept his invitation to Seattle, and if I talk to him, I just might.

A light breeze caresses my skin, and the haunting call of an owl comes from a nearby tree.

I could stretch out the writing for days, weeks, or months. I could stay forever, but my conscience won't allow it. Maybe it's not my conscience, but Emma wanting to find her way back.

After a long time on the porch, I return to Emma's bedroom and sit down at the computer, wiping a tear off my cheek. I have to be steadfast and brave. It's time to finish the story and let Emma reclaim her life.

CHAPTER 51

T he sheriff doesn't make any noise as I leave him to bleed out in his trap.

Barely able to walk, I stagger through the woods toward the gravel road. My legs wobble and threaten to crumple beneath me. The struggle with Travis has zapped any energy I had left. My right eye is swollen shut where his elbow smashed into my face.

I shudder, imagining him clawing his way out of the pit and coming after me. No. That's impossible. He's finished and so is his reign of terror.

My body begs to lie down, but I won't. Emma's life depends on me, and I will deliver. The most dangerous part of our escape may be behind us, but we won't survive if I give in to weakness now, succumbing to hypothermia and death. I force myself to keep going, one agonizing step after another. Every so often, I look back to ensure no one is coming after me.

Finally, I reach the end of the dirt road. The sight of the pavement ahead makes me cry out in giddy laughter.

Through my one good eye, I see a solitary streetlight in the distance. The paved road is just as deserted as the dirt road behind me. I'm unsure of which direction to take. Which way will lead to safety before my body gives out?

A distant sound cuts through the silence. I don't trust my senses. Hypothermia plays tricks with your mind and can make you hallucinate. But the noise persists and grows louder. It's real. An engine. Headlights come around a curve, cutting through the darkness. A vehicle is coming my way. This is my one chance, and I can't waste it. I must reach the road before it's too late.

With whatever strength remains in my feeble muscles, I stagger into the road. A pickup truck hurtles toward me. Raising my shaking hands into the blinding light, I face either rescue or a quick end.

The screech of brakes fills the night.

CHAPTER 52

I remember what happened next, though I was no longer in control. I remember through the lens of Emma's experiences and details shared by her parents, the psychiatrists, and the nursing staff. I don't need to write these chapters for Emma. She's already familiar with this part. But I want to. I'm not ready to let go yet. I'll do what I can to stay a little longer. Just one or two more chapters. I promise these will be the last.

FROM THE MANUSCRIPT

In the ICU, Nurse Julia Jefferson and her colleague Miranda Cox spoke in whispers near the mystery woman's bed.

The new patient's hair hung in long strands around her gaunt face. Her body was emaciated and frail, with fresh scratches marking her skin. A darkening bruise surrounded one eye as if someone had recently punched her hard. Julia had already cleaned and treated the physical wounds. The woman now slept soundly.

"When did she come in?" Miranda asked.

"At the start of our shift," Julia answered.

"She an addict?"

"Tox screen will tell us. Looks like she's been living outside. But she couldn't have been. Not this time of year. And her clothes were clean, mostly. Men's clothes. Way too big for her. She's been sleeping like the dead since she arrived."

Miranda leaned closer. She loved to learn patients' stories and always wanted to know more, especially with strange cases like this one. "Police pick her up? Or did someone drop her here?"

"Hunters found her on Miller's Gap Road. Said she walked right in front of them like a zombie. Nearly gave the guys a heart attack and got herself killed. She gave them a name—Katya—and a phone number for her parents before she collapsed. No cell service out there, so they brought her straight in."

"They stick around?"

"Nope. Left the second they could. Makes you wonder."

"You think they did this?"

Julia shrugged. "When I was looking for an ID, I found an animal bone and newspaper clippings in her coat pockets. All the articles were about missing women." Julia lifted her brows. "She'll have some explaining to do when she wakes up."

"Any theories?"

Julia shook her head. "I'll call her parents."

As Julia waited for the call to connect, she wasn't sure what to expect. Would the woman's parents be frantic with worry, or had they long ago severed ties with a troubled daughter?

"Hello?" The man's voice sounded cautious.

"This is Nurse Julia Jefferson at Western Carolinas Medical Center." She paused, weighing her next words. "I believe we might have your daughter."

Julia heard a sharp intake of breath.

"Emma? Is it Emma? Is she okay? Can we talk to her?"

Julia gazed at her patient. "She said her name was Katya."

A painful silence followed. "Our daughter is Emma," he finally said. "She's been missing for months. She was last seen in the North Carolina mountains."

Now it was Julia's turn to gasp. She thought about the articles in the woman's pocket.

"Well, this woman, whoever she might be, has been through quite a lot in the past few months. She's sleeping now. The people who brought her here said her name was Katya, but she *did* give them your phone number. She hasn't spoken yet. We didn't find any identification on her."

"Can you describe her?" the man asked.

"It would be better if you described your daughter to me," Julia told him, though she wondered if a woman who disappeared months ago would look anything like herself now.

"Emma is five foot six. When we last saw her, she weighed approximately one hundred and twenty-five pounds. Her hair is dark brown. Long. No curl to it. Brown eyes. Also, she has a birthmark on her neck."

The woman in the bed couldn't weigh more than a hundred pounds. Her dark hair was thin and matted against the pillow. Julia couldn't tell if it was straight or not. The woman's eyes remained closed.

"What kind of birthmark?" Julia asked, moving closer to the patient.

"Like a dog's paw print. It's small, smaller than a dime."

Julia aimed her penlight at the woman's neck. She saw it. Four faint brown marks arranged like a paw print. It was small enough that she'd missed the mark earlier because she wasn't looking for it. "I see it! On the left side of her neck. I think we have your daughter."

"You do? It's Emma? You have Emma? Oh, my God! Yes! Tell her we're coming for her."

CHAPTER 53

FROM THE MANUSCRIPT

My first coherent thought is my name. Emma Wilson.

Tubes protrude from my arms. For one terrible moment, I'm convinced my captivity has evolved into some twisted medical experiment. There's a curtain surrounding my bed, hanging from the ceiling, but it's not the same ceiling I've been staring at for months. I'm no longer in the dreadful basement.

My worn clothes are gone, replaced by a thin gown. A hospital gown. I'm in a hospital. I want to cry with relief, but another terror strikes me. I have no memory of coming here. The last thing I recall is being in that basement, losing hope, and slipping away. Then, nothing until now. This must be a dream. It has to be, except everything seems so real—the antiseptic smell, the aching all over my body, the clean sheets against my skin.

I hear voices. Two women. Their shadows move behind the curtain. They're speaking to each other in low, calm voices. They're real, too.

"Excuse me." My voice is so weak, I have to try again. "Excuse me."

Their conversation stops, and the curtain slides to one side. A woman in scrubs appears, her expression kind and professional. "You're awake," she says in a soothing tone. "Hello. I'm a nurse. You're in the hospital."

I struggle to focus on her name tag, Julia Jefferson, R.N., but even her reassuring presence can't quiet my fear. I may be in a safer place now, but how did I get here? The gap in my memory aches like an open wound.

"My name is Emma Wilson," I blurt. "I was abducted."

"We know," she says. "You're safe now. Your parents are on the way. But first, let's check you over again."

After undergoing another round of medical checks and devouring a warm meal of buttered pasta with a little parmesan cheese and green beans, my first normal meal in months, Julia helps me move to a private room. I drift in and out of sleep until my parents arrive.

They break down as they hold me, their tears mixing with mine. They don't bombard me with questions. I'm not sure if they're worried about my strength or if they're protecting themselves from the horrors I might reveal. Either way, I'm grateful I don't have to explain where I've been and what I've endured. I'm not ready. Some memories of my captivity are painfully vivid, but there's a lot I don't remember.

"All that matters is that you're okay now," my mother says.

She's wrong. I'm alive, yes. I'm physically safe. I'm free from the hunter. But I'm still afraid, and I'm not "okay."

"We're going to get whoever did this to you, whoever took you from us," my father says. "The police are on their way, if you're ready to talk."

Terror shoots through me. I bolt upright, jerking the lines attached to my arm. "You called the police?"

"The hospital did," he says. "What's wrong?"

"The man who took me—he's the sheriff!"

My mother tightens her arms around me, and my father tenses.

"Don't worry. No one is going to hurt you now. I won't let that happen," my father promises. "I'll be right back."

He leaves the room, but my mother stays. She hugs me, and we cry. I'm relieved but also overwhelmed with confusion because of my memory gap.

Later, Detective Nadine Smith arrives. She's a female police officer, thanks to my parents' insistence.

My parents remain in the room, flanking me like protective guards. I begin my terrible story with, "The sheriff abducted me." I describe the basement room with the tally marks others left on the wall and the hunting escapades. My parents try to hide their shock as they grip each other.

My battered, undernourished condition backs up my story. Detective Smith treats me with empathy and compassion, and I'm certain she believes me. When I've told her everything I can remember about my captivity, she asks, "How did you escape?"

The question I've been dreading. I've been thinking about my escape since I regained consciousness, expecting I'd remember soon, but there's still nothing there. Perhaps the sheriff had drugged me again and abandoned me by a main road. It's just hard to believe he would do that, knowing I could lead the authorities right to him. Also, that explanation doesn't fit with what the nurse shared about my arrival here. The people who brought me in said I walked into the middle of the road holding my arms up. I don't remember that either. My memory is a gaping void stretching from my last recollection of the sheriff taunting me until I woke up in the hospital.

"I'm sorry. I can't remember," I tell her.

The detective's voice is kind. "That's okay. It might come to you soon. You told your rescuers your name was Katya. Does that mean anything to you?"

"No." A quick shake of my head follows. The name resonates with me, but only in the context of the Zipporah Bazile *Darkness* novels, where Katya Strauss is the heroine. But that's fiction, not reality. In real life, I don't know anyone by that name.

The detective allows me time to think before posing her next question. "The newspaper articles in your pocket, about the missing women—where did those come from?"

Another blank. "Articles?"

Detective Smith shows no signs of impatience and clarifies with, "Articles cut from newspaper print. You had them with you."

"I can't tell you anything about articles cut from a newspaper. I'm sorry."

She shows me an evidence bag with newspaper clippings. One is older and more yellow than the others. I glimpse the sheriff's face on the newsprint and look away, nausea rising.

"I've never seen those papers, but that's him. That's the man who took me and kept me in the basement of his cabin."

"Do you know where he is now?"

"No."

The detective's eyes narrow. "The clothes you were wearing when you got here. Men's clothes. Do those belong to the sheriff?"

I shake my head. "I don't remember putting on anyone else's clothes."

Detective Smith shares a loaded expression with my parents before turning back to me. "I'm sorry you went through this, and I'm glad you got out of it alive. Get some rest. We'll talk more tomorrow."

I hope everything will make sense tomorrow. My mind will fill in the troubling gaps in my memory.

"You're going to arrest that monster now?" my father asks, more of a demand.

Detective Smith nods. "Yes, sir. I'll contact you when we have him."

The sheriff's arrest can't come soon enough. I must know he's behind bars where he can't hurt me or anyone else again.

CHAPTER 54

I t's the middle of the night. The house is silent as I sit at Emma's desk, staring at the last page I wrote. Poor Emma. All this time, she's lived in fear of the sheriff coming back for her. I should have found a way to tell her then, but at least I have now. When she reads the manuscript, she'll know she's truly safe.

With a lump forming in my throat, I consider my parting words. I hit return twice and begin typing a personal message at the end of the story. It's my advice for Emma.

The story is yours to revise or continue. If you want my opinion, delete it all and move on. You should own every bit of your life, make every decision, and choose every word. You are stronger than you think, and you're also an excellent writer. Neither Zip nor I could exist without you.

After closing the document, I compose a separate email I want Emma to read first, before she sees anything else.

Hi, Emma. This is Katya, one of your alter-personalities. This must be frightening since you don't know me, but I know you, and I promise you can trust me.

I got us out of the wretched basement last year. I don't possess all your writing and editing skills, but to the best of my ability, I've written that part of your story. The manuscript is attached here. If you read it, you'll understand how you escaped. I haven't shown the chapters I wrote to anyone else. They're only for you.

Best wishes and good luck. I'm always here if you need me,

Love, Katya.

When I've written and revised the email several times, I wait before pressing send. I don't have to do this yet. There's no rush. I can stay a few more days. A few more weeks. The thought tempts me like a powerful addiction, but moving on is the right thing to do. Emma needs to reclaim her life. I've done what I came to do to make that happen. I protected her and shared the truth about her escape. I also showed her an inner strength she doesn't yet realize she has.

Each of my movements is slow and deliberate as I tear a sheet from Emma's monogrammed notepaper and leave her a third and final message. This one could have gone into the email or at the end, but it deserves to stand alone. The other messages are about our past. This note is about Robert and Emma's future.

When I've chosen the right words for this important note, I place the paper on her bedside table, weighing it down with her phone. I take off my necklace with the raven pendant, a reminder of everything that happened at Raven's Hollow. Gently, I set it down with the note.

In the bathroom, I wash up, then rearrange Emma's toiletries the way she likes them. Taking my time, I rub her favorite coconut butter lotion over my feet and hands, then change into her favorite sleep shirt and shorts with the soft, silky fabric.

Tears blur my vision as I slide between the sheets and stare at the shadows on the ceiling. The owl outside emits a sad and eerie call that matches my mood. But this is right and necessary. Emma is ready now.

Finally, I close my eyes and surrender to the fade, knowing I'll always be a part of her strength.

PART III

EMMA

CHAPTER 55

Consciousness returns as if I'm emerging from a deep sleep. It's like I'm trapped inside a dream with layers, and each one needs to be peeled back before I can climb through. When I finally open my eyes and blink, I'm in my room. Not in my apartment, but in my parents' house. The place I moved back into because they were too worried about me being alone. Unfortunately, I remember the reason. My abduction.

My ordeal is branded in my memory like a hideous scar. A year has passed, and I'm still not okay. I've avoided even the simplest of tasks, like getting out of bed.

Sounds come from downstairs. The clatter of a pan as it's wrestled from the pile of cookware beneath the stove, and my father's voice. If he's home, it must be a Saturday or Sunday.

My poor parents. Guilt hits me because of the trouble I've caused them. They're worried about me, and for their sake, I have to work against the overwhelming desire to pull the covers up to my chin and go back to sleep. I'm not proud of staying in bed most of the day, but I can't stop myself either.

If I have a session with Donna today, it will be more of the same. She believes that unlocking my subconscious memories and facing them is the key to my recovery, but every time I dredge up the details of my captivity, another piece of me seems to wither away and die. Every attempt chips away another piece of me. I'm becoming less whole each time I try.

But I will try again. Everyone, myself included, wants to know how I got away from that cabin. I can't fathom how I did it without assistance. Yet no one has come forward claiming to have helped me. No one else knew I was there.

The sheriff is still on the loose. That knowledge poisons everything. The not knowing is terrible. I'm haunted by the fear that he'll return for me. I'm afraid to be with people but also terrified to be alone.

It's been a year since I met anyone new. When it comes to men, I don't think I'll ever trust them.

My parents' voices drift up again. I sigh beneath the covers. I must get up and put my feet on the floor. I have to go downstairs and say good morning or good afternoon, whatever it is. I have to try.

This morning seems different. I feel like I've slept for ages, but my head pounds as if I was up all night. What did I do? Considering I've hardly left the house except for walks and therapy, I have no explanation.

Rolling onto my side, I struggle to remember the events of last night. There's nothing. Not just yesterday, but the whole previous week is gone. I don't remember anything except my last session with Donna, which seems like it happened weeks ago, although that can't be right.

A jolt of fear strikes me. This isn't the first time I've lost a huge chunk of time. Has something happened, something so terrible my mind had to block it out to protect me again? I need to know, for my family's sake, if nothing else.

I slide my phone off the bedside table. A piece of notepaper and a lightweight metal object fall to the floor, but I don't search for them. I'm focused on my phone. It's almost nine a.m.

I force myself out of bed and straight into a hot shower. Emerging from the steam in a towel, I wipe condensation off the mirror and face my reflection. I have to wipe the mirror again to ensure I'm not imagining things. What I see is not what I expected. I don't just look different; I look better. Healthy. My eyebrows are shaped, and my face carries more fullness. My skin almost glows, and my nails are neat and trimmed with a clear coat of polish.

The transformation baffles me, but I'm not complaining. It's a start toward much-needed improvement. The visible changes should ease some of my parents' concerns. With that in mind, I get dressed and head downstairs.

The smell of sizzling bacon and frying eggs comes from the kitchen. My mother and father stand together at the stove.

"Morning," I say.

"Good morning," Dad answers, as Mom greets me with, "Hope you're hungry. We're preparing a big breakfast. We rarely cook bacon, but we saw how much you like it."

I stare at the pans, my head tilting in confusion. "You made me bacon? I don't understand." The words come out gentle, in bewilderment. I haven't touched meat in years, and bacon, of all things? I could deliver my usual passionate speech about pigs' intelligence and their emotional capacity beyond dogs. I was already a vegetarian, but after my captivity, I became even more sensitive to the plight of vulnerable beings. My parents know all this. So, what's going on?

They don't answer right away. Mom takes me in from head to toe, and I'm glad my appearance has improved. Her mouth quivers between a smile and a sob. She launches herself across the kitchen, wrapping me in a desperate embrace.

"Emma! Oh, Emma!" She hugs me hard, like she's afraid I'll vanish.

I'm even more confused now.

Dad's voice is thick with emotion. "Sweetheart, you left us for a while. You were gone."

A chill courses through me. "Gone?"

They keep staring at me. Words seem to fail them. I was right. Something happened. They either don't want to or can't explain it.

I escape my confusion by diving into the fridge, grabbing a yogurt container, and rummaging through the fruit drawer for blueberries. Such a normal thing to do, but when I turn back, they're watching me as if gathering the ingredients for my breakfast was an extraordinary feat.

"That's our Emma." Mom's voice quivers as she brushes hair from my face, tears welling in her eyes.

Unease crawls up my spine as I grab a bowl. They join me at the table with coffee, still watching, beaming.

"We have a lot to tell you, Emma," Dad says.

"Wait, Jack." Mom places her hand on his. "Not yet. Let's just have this peaceful breakfast first."

"Good idea." He's still smiling.

Something unusual is going on. Yet my parents seem so happy.

I stop eating and wind a strand of hair around my fingers. Whatever it is they're going to tell me, I'd better brace myself.

Only when Mom has topped our coffee mugs and sat down again does she fill me in. "What do you remember of the last three weeks?"

My foot taps uncontrollably under the table. "I don't remember any-thing."

Maybe in my depression, my brain sort of shut off, and I slipped into a coma. I bet my parents didn't know when I was going to wake up. Seeing the relief on their faces now, I'm so glad I did. I've been super depressed lately, but I don't want to die. I want to get better.

Mom gets up to hug me as I shake. "It's okay, Emma. It's okay."

"Tell me what happened." I'm expecting to hear a version of my new theory that they found me in a comatose state and kept vigil by my bedside.

"You know how your psychiatrists believed you had blocked certain memories?" Mom asks.

"Yes. I blocked out the memories my brain couldn't handle."

"Turns out, there was a lot more to it than that."

Another chill snakes down my spine. Whatever's coming, it's more shocking than a coma.

CHAPTER 56

I follow my parents into the seldom-used formal living room and sit beside my mother, facing the grand piano. My father sits across from us, perched on the edge of the armchair, leaning in and close enough to touch.

"Please tell me," I say.

Mom laces her fingers together, locking then unlocking her hands. This isn't easy for her.

"You know how one of your favorite authors is Zipporah Bazile?" she asks. "You've always felt some connection with her. Once you told us that you and she even share the same birthday."

"Yes." I can't imagine how those seemingly random statements relate to what happened to me.

My mother glances at my father as if she's not sure where to start. "A few weeks ago, I checked on you, like I always do."

I nod. Her morning checks are routine. They're gentle attempts to coax me out of bed and get me to act like a normal person.

"I heard the hair dryer, which was unusual because you hadn't been attentive to your appearance since you came back from the hospital. From the moment I saw you, I knew something had changed."

My forehead wrinkles in confusion. "Changed, how?"

"You'd just finished drying your hair. The next clue was your outfit. You were wearing a silk blouse and nice slacks. It had been so long since you'd gotten dressed like that without some prompting."

I glance down at what I'm wearing. Baggy sweats and an oversized sweatshirt that drowns my frame. Since the ordeal, I haven't cared about clothes or what I look like. I've slumped around in a mostly disheveled state.

My mom continues, "Then you said things that did not sound like you."

"What did I say?"

"You were going on about needing a facial and eyebrow wax, complaining about your nails. You said something like, 'Photographers could be anywhere. The longer I avoid the press, the more interested they become. I can't leave the house looking like this.' You sounded exasperated. Honestly, I didn't know what to think."

Neither do I. That doesn't sound like me. Not the person I was before, and especially not who I am now.

"You grabbed one of your Zipporah Bazile books and started talking about writing your next novel about a woman who gets abducted and held captive in a secluded cabin. You were adamant about needing a few weeks at a resort, a location that would inspire you and allow privacy. It became clear you believed you were Zipporah Bazile."

When I look at my father, he's nodding, his face grim.

"It was frightening, of course," Mom continues. "But apart from the obvious delusion, you were so confident and determined. You had new purpose. Getting yourself cleaned up and writing a book. We were relieved about that part, at least."

"How long ago was that?"

"Three weeks ago."

I rub my chin, taking time to think. I need to hear the story out. "Did I go to the doctors? Did they try to get me back to normal?"

"We called Donna and scheduled an urgent session. Zipporah referred to it as a meeting with her editor. When she described her ideas for her next book, Donna encouraged her to write it."

My jaw drops. I don't know whether to laugh or cry. The story turns stranger and creepier by the second. I did those things? Imagined I was a famous author?

"We pushed you so hard to remember what happened, your personality split into an alter. A new personality emerged as a coping mechanism. It's called dissociative identity disorder. For you, it resulted in memory gaps or blackouts," my mother says.

The explanation fits my experience, yet the idea of losing time to an alternate personality fills me with a paralyzing sense of panic. Suddenly, I'm extra sensitive to everything happening around me, every sound, everything I touch. I grip my hands together, clenching my jaw.

"Donna consulted with other experts. They also suggested we take a step back, to see what Zip would do."

"Zip?" I ask.

"That's what you called yourself."

It's getting hard to breathe. I bite the inside of my cheek and shift on the couch. "I don't remember any of this."

"Zip didn't seem to know anything about you either."

I listen with rapt attention, skin prickling with unease, as my parents share Zip's trip to Raven's Hollow in Colorado and how she behaved there. They tell me my best friend Sarah was so concerned that she also traveled to Raven's Hollow and stayed in the same guest wing. Zip didn't even recognize her.

My curiosity now rivals my fear. I have so many questions. As they recounted the past few weeks, one fact rose above all the other inconceivable information. In the world of Zipporah Bazile, I didn't seem to exist. She seized control, accepted my parents as hers while relegating me and my entire history to obscurity. Then she set to work, convinced she was a famous, bestselling author writing her next book. A story about my captivity.

"Zip was living my life until she left yesterday?" I ask.

"Not exactly," Mom says.

That's when they tell me about Katya.

CHAPTER 57

Alter personalities? Fragmentation? It's a lot to take in. In my wildest dreams, I did not see any of that coming.

In my room, not even my coziest sweater can banish the chill that's taken root inside me.

The only thing I remember about the last three weeks is what I just learned, which includes a trip to Raven's Hollow Resort. Everything else is a complete blank. The idea of my body operating independently of my will is so profoundly frightening it makes me shudder. I'm not alone. There are others. Not outside where I can shut the doors and lock them out, but hidden inside me, existing like cancers in remission. Or are they growing, getting stronger, preparing to take over again?

First, there's Zip. She sounded like a confident but paranoid woman. It's astonishing how she embraced her identity as *the* Zipporah Bazile. If she could access my memories, she'd know a lot about the author, at least about her novels. I've devoured and collected Bazile's books since her first book hit the shelves and all the bestseller lists. Zipporah Bazile as my alter-personality is bizarre, yet it also makes sense.

Then there's Katya, the all-knowing one, aware of Zip and me. She must be a product of everything I know about Katya Strauss from Bazile's *Darkness* series. My parents spoke of her as a guardian angel who had my back, a best friend I never knew I had. Someone who would do anything for me.

The hunters who brought me to the hospital said my name was Katya, and we all chalked it up to confusion on someone's part. We thought they might have misheard or misremembered. I might have mumbled incoherently as I passed out. With all that happened, it mattered little at the time. Now I know better. I have my explanation, and it's terrifying.

Despite how incredible it all sounds, I believe my parents. Their unwavering support has been my only constant, especially during the challenges of my "recovery." They'd never invent a wild story like that one. What purpose would that serve? However, I don't have to take their word alone. The evidence is waiting for me on my laptop.

My email inbox holds hundreds of unread messages, but one near the top grabs my attention. It got sent last night from my email address.

Someone else sat here and used my computer in my room while accessing my private thoughts. Not someone else, but something else, living inside my mind. I force my revulsion down. I can't let fear stop me from learning the truth. I have to accept the unnerving facts and move forward if I want to get better.

My hands shake as I summon the courage to read the email message I have no memory of sending.

Hi Emma. This is Katya, one of your alter-personalities. This must be frightening since you don't know me, but I know you, and I promise you can trust me.

I got us out of the wretched basement last year. I don't possess all your writing and editing skills, but to the best of my ability, I've written that part of your story. The manuscript is attached here. If you read it, you'll understand how you escaped. I haven't shown the chapters I wrote to anyone else. They're only for you.

Best wishes and good luck. I'm always here if you need me,

Love, Katya.

Katya says I can trust her, but her words don't quiet my churning stomach. A wave of nausea washes over me, and I think I might get sick.

Shaking inside, I click to open the attached document—*Untitled*. The manuscript is forty thousand words. More novella than novel, the editor in me automatically thinks.

I can't help wondering about the writing, and if it will be any good. My heart thumps wildly as I start reading.

The main character, Hannah, is undoubtedly me. The first few chapters aren't my exact abduction story, but close enough.

In Zip's chapters, I recognize the rhythm and flow of sentences and transitions I encourage as an editor. The grammar and punctuation are solid. Zip found all that inside me from the years I helped other writers. Even though I'm reading an account of the worst days of my life, it's still compelling. My eyes remain glued to the screen as I absorb each chapter.

I've been reading for over an hour, almost as if I'm in a trance, when I reach the point where Katya takes control. My face is mere inches from my screen. I'm trembling because from here on, I don't know what will happen next.

A knock on my open bedroom door makes me yelp in surprise.

Mom hovers in the doorway. "Sorry, Emma. I tried not to startle you. Just checking in."

"I'm okay for now. Just, you know, a little overwhelmed."

"I called Donna. She can meet with us this afternoon. I think we should see her."

"Wait, no. I don't want to talk to her yet. I found the manuscript. I'm reading it now."

"You are?" She clutches the door frame. "Would you like me to stay with you while you read it?"

"No, but thank you. I'm so grateful you and Dad are here with me. This is a lot."

"Yes, it is." She hesitates, unsure if she should leave. "I'll be downstairs, just a shout away if you need me."

"Okay. Thank you," I say again before she walks away, leaving the door ajar. Somehow, I just know it's best to read this alone before anyone else sees it.

Trying to keep calm, I dive back into the story.

Katya is a lot like her namesake from the *Darkness* novels. Fierce and unstoppable. As I read about her picking locks with bones, I'm impressed, yet the scene is familiar. I've read about her escaping from a basement room before. She did the same thing in a *Darkness* novel.

I keep reading. My hands are clenched into tight fists, fingernails piercing my skin, when she lures the sheriff into the pit. With her parting words, my horror mingles with relief and gratitude. He's gone. He's not out there waiting for a second chance to hurt me or anyone else. He can't come back.

Finally, I know the truth.

My head swirls with the enormity of it all. I wrote this story. Except, I didn't. I did the things Katya described doing, except I don't remember any of it. I'm not sure what that means. Am I responsible for a man's death or not? I didn't kill the sheriff, but I left him to die rather than get him help. If people learned the truth, would they consider it self-defense or murder? Or would I plead insanity?

I drop my head into my hands until I'm ready to read the last of the manuscript. Once I start again, I don't stop until I reach the end. The last few lines are separate, in a different font. They're not part of the story. It's a message from Katya.

Emma,

The story is yours to revise or continue. If you want my advice, delete it all and move on. You should own every bit of your life, make every decision, and choose every word. You are stronger than you think, and you're also an excellent writer. Neither Zip nor I could exist without you.

—Love, Katya.

For a long while, I sit alone and think.

The truth is on my laptop: I broke, and Katya emerged. It's all terrifying and fascinating.

Katya wants me to delete the story and move on.

I open the manuscript again, scrolling to the scene where she emerges. Now that I know what happened and the sheriff isn't coming back, I can heal. That's all that matters. No one else needs to know that I broke. They don't need to know about Katya or Zip.

My cursor is waiting on top of the file's icon. With one click, I can erase it all.

My finger trembles on the mouse. I'm still deciding.

I click and delete, and the document vanishes.

That's not enough.

I find it in the trash folder and delete it again. Permanent this time.

Like sadistic hunters at the bottom of pits, some things should stay buried.

CHAPTER 58

I'm still in my bedroom, just thinking. Mom knocks on the door again. My father is with her.

"Are you okay?" he asks.

I manage a smile. "I will be. I'm working on it."

Mom carries a tray of food—avocado toast, pepper slices, and almonds. "Thought you might be hungry."

Only then do I realize how much time has passed. It's late afternoon, long past lunch.

As Mom crosses the room, I spy the notepaper that fell from my bedside table this morning. It's still on the floor.

My parents sit down on the loveseat at the end of my bed.

"Did you read the story Katya left you?" Dad asks.

"I did. I know what happened now. I know how I escaped the cabin."

My mother clasps her hands under her chin. "You do? Oh. We'd like to read it if that's okay with you."

"I'm not sure that's a good idea. It's very personal."

"You're not going to share it?" my father asks, crossing and uncrossing his legs.

"I'd rather not. I think it's best. I hope you understand." It's a big deal to deny them the information when they've been wondering for so long, and I feel terrible about that, but I can't share it.

Their disappointment is clear, but for now, they don't push back.

My mother fiddles with the hem of her shirt. She does that when she's upset. "Sarah has been calling to ask about you every day. We let her know you returned. I'm sure she'll come over soon to see you."

"Okay. I'm eager to hear what she has to say about all this. I can't imagine what she thinks."

When they leave, my attention goes to the paper on the floor. I crouch to pick it up and find something else beside it, a necklace with a raven charm.

The note has handwriting, and it's not mine. The letters are larger and looser.

Hi, Emma, It's Katya. Check the recent pictures on your phone. Robert Yates is a great guy. I trust him. He thinks he spent ten days with you at Raven's Hollow Lodge and that you were initially pretending to be Zip for the sake of your novel. You had an excellent time together. He's waiting for you to call him and can't wait to see you again. His number is on your phone.

Robert Yates? My parents told me they went to the resort and kept watch over me, along with Sarah, but they mentioned nothing about a guy named Robert.

Biting the inside of my cheek again, I grab my phone from my desk and open my photo app. I've taken few pictures this past year, but my app holds pages of recent photos, none of which I recognize. I'm so freaked out that I drop the phone from my hand as if it's burning me.

It's too much, this additional evidence that someone invaded my life without my awareness. They've used my laptop and my phone, my body and my mind. I feel violated.

Deep breaths.

When I'm ready to face my weird reality again, I pick up my phone and study the photos. The first set of pictures captures stunning views of mountains, a valley of pine trees, and log-built chalet-style buildings. This must be Raven's Hollow. Interior shots follow. There's a huge bedroom with rustic decorations, a bathroom with a claw-foot tub and stones for shower tile. A common area has a massive stone fireplace. Next come photos of the meals I apparently ate, and I'm not thrilled to see various cuts of meat.

The first photo with me in it makes my adrenaline spike. It's the strongest proof that I existed in a dissociative state. In the image, I'm at Raven's Hollow, and I'm not alone. I'm with a handsome man. Presumably Robert Yates.

The photos are close-up selfies. In one with mountain bikes, my head leans against his chest. In another, our shoulders touch, heads tilted toward each other, smiles lighting our faces as we pose. We look like more than friends, yet until this moment, I've never laid eyes on him. That should deeply disturb me, and it does. But there's more to what I'm seeing.

My first memory gap represented an escape from horror, but this recent loss reveals the opposite. Something good. I look healthy and happy, and I haven't been either of those things in the past year. As I continue to study the picture, I long to feel that way again.

I hear voices downstairs.

Soon after, there's a tentative knock on my bedroom door, and then it opens.

Sarah peeks in, tilting her head, a small smile on her face.

"Hey, Sarah. It's me. Emma. Come on in."

Her smile spreads. "It's really you?"

"It's me." I barely get the words out before she races across the room and throws her arms around me.

"Oh my God," she says as I hug her back. "I missed you so much."

When she pulls away, she studies my face. "Are you okay? I mean, how are you?"

"I'm okay. I look better, don't I?" I laugh as I sink onto the loveseat in the corner of my room and pat the spot beside me. "I heard you went all the way to Colorado to keep an eye on me. Thank you."

"I wanted to be there for you."

"Tell me everything. How did I act as Zip?"

Sarah sits. "I was only there the first five days, but I spent as much time with you, I mean with Zip, as I could."

"What was she like?"

"She was confident. A little paranoid, though maybe because I was a stranger to her. She identified with your parents, but she didn't have any idea who I was. We took a yoga class together, and watching her, it was like I was in class with you, until she told me she'd never done yoga before. She believed it."

I grimace as I listen. "I'm not sure how you could see me like that and keep it together."

"It wasn't easy, but your doctors said it was best to let you go on as Zip and write the book. So, did it work? Did the book get written? Is that why you're back?"

"I think so."

"Do you know what happened, how you escaped the cabin?"

I nod.

Sarah stares at me, eyes wide, imploring me to tell her more. When I don't, she doesn't press.

"Did you meet a guy named Robert, by any chance?" I ask.

She grins. "Of course I did. I wasn't going to let you go off with a strange man. I vetted him for you. Grilled him, to be honest, when you weren't around. So, you remember him?"

"No. I saw pictures on my phone."

"I took a few of you together." She grins again. "He's kind and gorgeous, he has his life together, and he's completely smitten with you."

"We don't know if he's into me or my alter."

"She was still you. Part of you."

"I guess she must be. There's no other way."

"You and Robert got along great. He was so attentive. You had a *very* good time together." She stares at me.

I know that look. Suddenly my mouth is dry. I hope I'm misunderstanding her. "What did I do?'

Her smile quivers. "I think you slept with him, Emma. He stayed overnight in your room."

"Oh, my God." I could tell we were close from the photos, but I didn't imagine we were intimate. I cover my face with my hands, trying to process the information. I feel like I need a new body, this one is defiled.

"Are you okay?" Sarah asks.

"This is so strange. I can't even."

"I know. But I don't think you regretted it. I'm certain." Sarah rubs my back. "It's going to be okay. Whatever happened, I think it helped you. Extremely bizarre circumstances aside, you were happy."

I look up at her. "Does anyone else know? About my alter?"

"No. I haven't told a soul."

"Thank you. I'd like to keep it that way."

"That's why your parents agreed to your Raven's Hollow trip. Zip wanted to go, and it allowed you some privacy while you were... not yourself.

Your doctors were sure it would be a temporary state. Looks like they were right. And no matter who you are, I've got you. I've got your back."

I hug her again, truly grateful for her support.

Later, after Sarah leaves, I study all the photos on my phone again. I can't believe I slept with this guy, but I do look happy. I suppose, since we've already had sex, what's the harm in speaking with him on the phone.

I dial Robert's number before I lose my courage or talk myself out of it.

The phone rings twice. Someone answers. "Hey! You called! I survived the wait."

"Hi." I'm wavering between fear and fascination, close to hanging up and pretending I never called. "This is Emma."

Robert's laugh matches the smiling face from the photos. "I know. It's great to hear from you. I really missed you. I guess this means you finished your book. Congratulations!"

CHAPTER 59

D r. Payson crosses her legs in the leather chair facing me. She holds a notepad on her lap and grips a gold pen. Her horn-rimmed glasses rest below the bridge of her nose.

"I'm familiar with your medical history and background," she says. "Tell me why you switched psychiatrists."

I grip my blue notebook, rotating it in my hands. "Because you're an expert on dissociative disorders. Also, my last doctor might have pushed too hard for me to remember things. The more she pushed, the more I felt myself slipping. Then, someone else took over. I lost weeks of my life."

Dr. Payson writes a few lines in her book. "That must have been frightening."

"It was. Is. I mean, I didn't know it was happening, but I don't want it to happen again."

"Your alters didn't exist until your mind reached its breaking point. Whoever they are, whatever they're capable of, they came from within you. They're part of you."

"I know, but I'd prefer they don't come back. Especially Zip. She wanted to erase me."

"Based on what I know, I don't think that's true, Emma. She wanted to erase your weakness and self-doubt. The things that were preventing you from achieving your full potential. She wanted you to be a stronger version of yourself."

"I like that explanation better, but I still don't want her coming back."

Dr. Payson sets her notepad aside. "We can work on prevention strategies. Particularly on strengthening your present self."

"How?"

"Start with a mantra. For example, I am present, I am whole, I am in control. You'll want to make it yours. Choose words that resonate with you and bring you comfort."

After writing the words down, I repeat them.

"Don't just say your mantra. Own it. For example, when you say present, note where you are." She gestures to encompass her office, then places her hand over her heart. "When you say whole, breathe in and feel your chest expanding. For control, sit up taller, contract your abs, and feel your inner strength."

I try again with the words, letting each one connect to a physical sensation.

"Good. Tell me, when do you feel most vulnerable to an alter?"

I swallow as I think of my response. "When I'm stressed. Or when people ask about when I escaped." My voice drops. "Sometimes, I get this strange ripple inside."

"A ripple? Can you be more specific?"

"I don't know how to explain it. It's just like something is off. As soon as it happens, I panic. I'm worried an alter-personality is trying to surface."

"And this happens every time you get stressed?"

I press my hands into my thighs and rock forward. "Maybe not every time."

"When something isn't right, instead of worrying, start with your mantra."

"And if it doesn't work?"

"Ground yourself further with this three-two-one exercise. Identify three things you can see. Two you can touch. One you can hear." She demonstrates, pointing out objects on her walls. The material of her blouse. The quiet hum of the air conditioning. "The exercise forces your brain to engage with the external world. It helps connect you to the present."

I'm not sure it will help, but it's easy enough. I have to trust Dr. Payson knows what she's doing.

"Don't let the fear of your alters consume you. That creates the stress that can trigger dissociation. Instead, build a solid foundation for yourself."

"Right. That's what I'm trying to do."

"What makes you feel most alive?"

"Writing. I've been editing for years. Now I'm finally writing a novel."

"Excellent. What are you writing about?"

"It's fiction. A thriller."

"Good. What else do you enjoy?"

"I'm currently in a relationship with a guy named Robert. I love spending time with him. He doesn't know about the alters, though."

"Do you plan on telling him at some point?"

"I don't know."

"We can cross that bridge when the time comes, and I can help you through that. Meanwhile, have a plan for each day, including things you want to accomplish. The stronger your present identity, the less space for others to emerge."

"Only a few people know about the alters, and I want to keep it that way."

Dr. Payson dips her head. "I understand. I'm not at liberty to share your identity."

Fortunately, I can rely on the discretion of those who know. My psychiatrists are bound by patient-doctor confidentiality, and my parents are devoted to my best interests. Robert still believes Zip was simply a part of my creative process at Raven's Hollow. Sarah knows, but I trust her. She's earned my confidence again and again. I'm so lucky to have a friend like her.

I leave Dr. Payson's office with my new list of techniques and a commitment to focus on my present self.

When I get home, I return to revising my novel. The story Zip and Katya wrote is gone, and I'm writing a new version. Until the point where I broke, the overall story hasn't changed much. I've simply strengthened it in the rewriting. After that, I made significant alterations. Now the novel is part truth, part fiction, and every word is mine.

There's no shattering. No emerging alters. No gruesome death. Just one woman who found her strength when she needed it most, and then she escaped.

"I am present," I whisper, my gaze moving over the words, sentences, and paragraphs I reclaimed. "I am whole," I say louder, breathing deep, then sitting up taller. "I am in control."

CHAPTER 60

Nine months later

I'm about to shower after taking a yoga class when my literary agent's text fills my screen. *Major publishers are interested. Bidding war potential.*

I reply with a thumbs-up emoji.

She responds, *Given your story, we could market this as true crime. Your ordeal would drive massive interest. Unless you're more comfortable with fiction.*

I type out the same thing I've already told her. *It has to be fiction. I want to publish under a pen name and market the book as a psychological thriller.*

As soon as I hit send, a stirring sensation inside me makes my muscles tense. I grip my desk. "I am here. I am safe. I am Emma," I say, shifting my gaze from one object to the next until the sensation fades.

My agent's reply comes quickly: *Are you sure? Your real-life story made national headlines. This could be your chance to tell the world.*

I write back: *I'm one hundred percent sure. Fiction.*

Most of it *is* fiction.

In my version of the story, Katya never existed. I have faith she'd never hold that against me. She's the reason I got out of there alive and I'm again productive and as healthy as I can be, considering all that has happened. She encouraged me to contact Robert, and now I have a wonderful relationship with him.

Despite my continued work with Dr. Payson, I occasionally experience that internal rippling. I think it's Zip, and she's telling me the book is hers, not mine. Dr. Payson disagrees. She believes it's only me doubting my writing abilities, which is normal for authors. In Dr. Payson's professional opinion, Zip didn't want to eliminate me when she was in control. She only wanted to erase my weakness and self-doubt.

Without Zip, the first draft of my novel wouldn't exist. Naturally, I'm thinking about her more now that I'm discussing the book's publication. It's exciting but also stressful, so I repeat my mantra for good measure. "I am here. I am safe. I am Emma."

"Did you say something?" Robert asks from the bathroom doorway, making me jump.

"Just rehearsing what I should tell my agent." I manage a smile. Robert doesn't know about Katya and what happened to the sheriff. He only knows the version of the story I've put into the new book.

He wraps his arms around me, and I lean into his body.

"You're going with the pen name?" he asks.

"Definitely. I don't want to be known as the victim who wrote a book. I want the story to stand on its own."

Fiction means I control which truths to tell. Fiction means no one else ever needs to know my darkest and strangest secrets.

CHAPTER 61

Eighteen months later

U nder bright studio lights on the television stage, I sit across from talk show host Lesley Coolidge and try to keep my hands still in my lap.

Lesley makes animated hand gestures as she introduces me with her bubbly voice. "We're here with author Emma Wilson discussing her debut novel *When She Escaped*. The recent response to this novel has been pretty incredible."

"Overwhelming," I say, grasping the raven charm around my neck to anchor myself as a strange sensation ripples through me.

"To recap, your publisher released *When She Escaped* under a pseudonym. No one knew it was you who wrote it."

"That's right."

Lesley rubs her hands together. "Fans of dark suspense novels loved the chilling atmosphere you created. They thought you described the captivity convincingly, almost as if you had lived it."

I nod and offer a slight smile.

"Then... " she pauses for dramatic effect, leaning toward me. " ...somehow the news leaked that your novel was based on a true story. That's all it took for *When She Escaped* to become an overnight sensation. And perhaps that's the silver lining to your experience. Your literary success. But such a harrowing story. I'm so sorry you had to go through it."

"So am I. It was horrible."

"And you weren't the first victim. You were the third woman that monster locked in his basement."

"The third that we know of. When my captor—"

Lesley holds up her hand to stop me. "I'm sorry to interrupt." She turns to stare into an off-stage camera. "Spoiler alert for those of you who haven't read the book yet, though most of you tuning in to my show already have. Are you ready for this? Emma's captor was the local sheriff!"

Murmurs of outrage come from the studio audience.

"Cover your ears if you don't want to hear how she escaped because that's what we're about to discuss." Lesley faces me again, her eye contact strong. "Tell us how it happened. And how did you feel when you knew you were finally getting away?"

"The sheriff was gone when I got my chance. And it was terrifying. I worried he might return any second and throw me back into the basement."

"And oh, my dear God, the way you got yourself out of that basement room. Asking for meat again and again even though you were a vegetarian. Just hoping he would bring you bones so you could use them as tools. So resourceful! I mean, girl, who would think of that? Just brilliant!"

"I didn't have other options. And it wasn't my original idea. I read about it in a book by Zipporah Bazile. Her character, Katya Strauss, uses bones to escape from a dungeon."

"Bazile is the author of the *Darkness* novels, right? Just fabulous! I haven't read them. I watched the Netflix series. I wonder if Zipporah Bazile knows she played a role in saving your life?"

I smile and shake my head.

"You escaped and walked miles in the cold to the main road—and you were not in good shape, girl, you were literally starving. And that's where some kind-hearted strangers found you."

"I'm forever grateful they drove by when they did."

"Even though you escaped, what makes this story especially disturbing is that law enforcement never found the sheriff. The theory is that he made a run for it after he discovered you'd escaped. According to true crime theorists, the sheriff knew his reign of terror would eventually end. They believe he had unregistered vehicles hidden somewhere, along with fake IDs, and another secluded cabin in some far-flung corner of the wilderness."

"Yes, that's what they think."

"Except, they found his dog inside the cabin. Strange that he would leave his dog behind, don't you think?"

"The guy was pure evil. Nothing he did could surprise me now."

When Detective Smith went to arrest the sheriff, she found Bolton barely conscious. If crime techs had run a toxicology panel on him, they would have discovered he'd ingested a hefty dose of sleeping medicine. The Detective took the dog home with her. Later, she adopted him. He's fine now.

"That horrible man is still out there somewhere," Lesley says, eyes gleaming.

I will not admit the truth. Not to Lesley. Not to anyone. If Katya is to be trusted—and I do trust her—the sheriff's body is rotting at the bottom of a pit somewhere in the miles of dense forest surrounding his home.

For an instant, I look beyond Lesley to Robert, who is waiting for me in the studio wings. He's rooting for me, his expression filled with pride. Seeing him gives me an extra boost of confidence. I guide the conversation away from my captivity and toward the process of writing.

I spend the rest of the interview discussing my editing background and my long-held dream of becoming an author.

Finally, Lesley concludes the segment by holding a hardback copy of my book in the air. The studio audience applauds, and someone to my left shouts, "Cut. That's a wrap."

The production crew escorts me offstage, where I join Robert.

"You did great up there. I'm so proud of you." He follows up with a kiss.

I lean my head against his chest, feeling his body, the fabric of his sports coat between my fingers, and the thump of his heart beneath my ear.

"I can't wait to have you all to myself at Raven's Lodge. Ready to head to the airport?" he asks.

"As ready as I'll ever be."

CHAPTER 62

Now that my book is out and the sheriff's deeds are public information, there's something I have to do for myself—make Raven's Hollow mine. Not through photos, but through my own experiences. That's why I'm here.

Fresh snow blankets the resort, making me shiver. For an instant, the scene transports me back to the secluded cabin.

Robert's voice returns me to the present. "It's totally different in winter, isn't it?"

Sunlight glints off the pristine white surfaces, almost blinding in intensity. I shield my eyes from the glare, fighting the sensation I've stepped into someone else's dream. Gripping the railing, I climb the stairs leading to the main lodge.

Robert holds the door open for me. "When we were last here, I had to work a lot at night, and you spent most of your trip writing," he says. "I'm glad you don't have the pressure of a deadline this time."

"I still met you, didn't I?" I tease, stepping inside and removing my heavy coat. In truth, I am planning another book. I'm just waiting for the right idea to come along, a concept I'm passionate about. Raven's Hollow might give me inspiration.

"Now that you're a famous author, I won't give your name. Respecting your privacy," Robert says, smiling.

He draws me in for a kiss, and for a moment, it's like we're the only people in the world even though we're in the lobby and just a few steps from the registration desk. Eventually, we part to get checked in.

"Reservation for Robert Yates," he says. "We're a little early."

The woman behind the desk, Jerrel, beams at us. "Good afternoon, Mr. Yates. You requested a specific suite. If it's ready, we can release it for you. Let me check."

As Jerrel consults her tablet, I look around the cozy, sophisticated lobby and a déjà vu sensation washes over me. I'm not sure whether it's a memory surfacing, if it's related to photos I've seen, or if it's something else.

"They're just finishing the preparations for your room," Jerrel says. "If you'd like to have a drink at the bar, it should be ready soon."

"A drink, then?" Robert asks me.

"Sure."

Jerrel gestures toward the rear of the lobby. "The Summit Bar is in this building. Just head to your left and you'll see the signs."

"Thanks. We know the way," Robert tells her.

We leave our luggage in the lobby, and I walk beside Robert to the bar. At the entrance, I say, "I'm just going to head to the restroom for a minute."

In the bathroom, I stare into the large, ornate mirror. I do my mental exercises and tell myself I'm strong and I've got this.

When I rejoin Robert, he's sitting on a bar stool at the counter with two drinks in front of him.

Mine is dark purple, almost black, with a blackberry and a tiny green leaf rimming the glass.

Robert raises his drink and offers a toast. "Here's to getting everything we want out of our vacation at Raven's Hollow."

I clink my glass against his. "Cheers to that."

He chuckles and there's a twinkle in his eyes. "Does that ring any bells?"

I smile back at him, tilting my head. I don't understand what he means.

"That was the toast I made the first time we came here. Don't you remember?" He grins, not a hint of reproach detectable. "No worries. I don't blame you. The night we met, I knew you were special. I wanted to make a good first impression and thought long and hard about that toast while the bartender was mixing our drinks. I was aiming for clever and memorable. Maybe it was clever enough, but it wasn't memorable."

"I'm sorry I don't remember the toast, but I promise you made a good impression."

"And I'm thankful for that."

There's no doubting his appreciation. I never have. From day one, he's been fully invested in our relationship.

Raising the glass to my lips, I take a sip and frown. The flavor of black licorice takes me back to my childhood—memories of eating black jelly-beans by mistake and spitting them out. I set the drink down quickly and place my hand over my mouth so he can't see my grimace.

Robert is more in tune with me than I realize. "What's wrong?" he asks.

My grimace turns to an apologetic laugh. "My drink tastes like black licorice. People either like it, or they hate it. I'm firmly in the hate group."

Robert signals the bartender over. "I ordered a Raven's Elixir. This one has licorice in it."

The bartender nods. "Absinthe."

"Is that a new ingredient you weren't using before?" Robert asks.

The bartender places both hands on the bar and leans into it. "That drink is one of our signature specials. We haven't changed the recipe. I can mix another and leave the absinthe out."

"Sure. I would appreciate that," I say.

Robert frowns. "I ordered the Raven's Elixir because it was your favorite drink the last time we were here."

I shrug. "Sorry."

"Don't apologize. People change. And maybe this bartender doesn't know what he's talking about," he whispers.

I try to return his smile as he moves to kiss me, but my doubts are creeping in. Maybe coming here wasn't such a great idea. What else might Zip or Katya have done at this place that I wouldn't have done? Ordering a drink I don't like isn't a big thing, but bigger surprises might await me. I wish I knew about my alters' activities the way Katya did.

Robert takes my hand. "You continue to amaze me. Sometimes you're fiery and bold, and sometimes you're quiet and thoughtful, but each version of you is captivating."

If that's what he thinks, I can live with it. I'm glad he appreciates every side of me.

With my drink replaced, we go over the activities we've planned. We're going skiing and ice skating, two things Zip and Katya didn't do with Robert in the summer.

After finishing our drinks, we're back at the front desk, and our suite is ready. Jerrel hands us the keys, and we follow a bellhop out of the lobby. All the paths are cleared but lined with sparkling walls of snow. We pass three gas fire pits on our way. I imagine sitting around them and toasting marshmallows, a cute activity the resort encourages by providing all the supplies. Maybe I'll suggest we try it.

Inside the Elk Lodge building, Robert says, "There's my room."

"Right," I say as if I remember, but there's nothing familiar about this hallway. It wasn't in the photos.

He unlocks the door to our suite, and I step into a room I'm only familiar with from pictures on my phone.

Robert goes to the balcony windows and looks out at the snow-covered mountains.

I sidle up to him and wrap my arms around his waist. He pulls me closer, and we admire the landscape together.

A raven lands on the balcony railing a few feet away from us. Its black feathers contrast with the snow. Its beauty is mesmerizing until it lets out a piercing shriek. As it flies away, a wave of dizziness washes over me.

"You okay?" Robert asks as I lean into him.

"I'm a little lightheaded. Must be the altitude."

"I'll put our things away. Just rest," he says. "We have the massages tonight. Remember how great those were?"

I force my lips into what I hope passes for a smile, but an uneasy fluttering sensation persists. To stay present, I fall back on my grounding exercises. Three things I see: the painting of horses and cowboys, the coffee maker with chrome accents, and the console made of burled wood. I touch the soft comforter and the smooth headboard. I hear Robert asking me which dresser I prefer.

I think I'm fine, it's just the altitude. I try to stay calm, but it's hard when this place holds so many memories that aren't mine.

CHAPTER 63

Bundled up in our coats and gloves, Robert and I take a brisk walk to the spa. We couldn't get massage appointments at the same time. Mine is first. His is right after.

Once we get there, I change into the resort's plush robe and slippers and pour a cup of their specialty tea. Sipping the herbal drink, I settle on a leather couch in front of a fireplace and watch the flickering flames.

Before Robert can join me, a woman calls from the back of the room. "Emma Wilson."

I rise to my feet and greet my masseuse.

"I'm Heidi," she says, looking at me with a peculiar expression. "I remember you."

"You do? I was here, but that was almost two years ago. It's incredible you would remember me."

"Absolutely." There's something a little off about her tone. "You got up in the middle of the massage and left. No explanation. That's never happened to me, and I've been doing this for ten years."

"I'm sorry." There's nothing else I can say. I don't know if Zip or Katya left, or why.

She leads me to the massage room and then steps out so I can take off my robe and lie down. When she returns, the lights dim, and quiet background music plays. It's all very serene, yet I'm stuck wondering what happened the last time my body was lying on this table.

A vanilla and pine fragrance fills the room, and Heidi kneads my back.

The massage is wonderful. The pressure is just right. I can't imagine anyone leaving before it's over. My tension unravels thread by thread. This is exactly what I needed.

Somewhere between the patterns of rhythmic, soothing strokes, I drift away as if I'm floating.

Then it comes—that ripple.

I sit up, touching the warm blanket and the solid table, smelling the candle's fragrance, and hearing the music.

As fast as it came, the sensation disappears, and I'm fine. Better than fine.

Finally, I understand what I'm feeling. I sense my alters when I'm stressed, but also when I'm relaxed and my consciousness is drifting, when I'm not trying to fight them.

I remember what happened in this same massage room two years ago. I tried to break through, but I wasn't strong enough. I wasn't ready to come back. Now, I don't need to leave. Thanks to my alters, I have every reason to stay and no reason to hide.

Before, when I felt those ripples, I panicked. Not anymore. My alters aren't separate from me. They're part of me. My brain created them to help me, not haunt me.

I'm ready to accept them.

"Are you all right?" Heidi asks.

"I'm good. Sorry about that. Just needed a minute." I turn back over and the session resumes.

When I leave the massage room, I find Robert sitting in the space I left. He's relaxed with his head tipped back. I stop in the doorway to watch him and realize I'm smiling.

I have so many reasons to be grateful. Without Katya's courage, I might not have lived to experience any of this. Beyond survival, I owe my amazing boyfriend and bestselling novel to Zip and Katya's confident spirits and their willingness to take risks.

Robert turns to find me watching him. Right away, he's at my side, his hand on my shoulder. "How are you?"

There is so much love and concern there, it makes me want to cry.

"Wonderful. I feel amazing." I stand on my tiptoes to plant a kiss on his lips. It starts tender and turns into something more electric as he kisses me back.

When we finally move apart, he stares deep into my eyes. "I can't stop thinking about meeting you here, and everything since. I love you so much, Emma."

A surge of warmth floods my body. "I love you, too." I wave my hand toward the massage rooms. "It's your turn. Go ahead. I'll be here, waiting. I promise I'm not going anywhere."

I pour myself another cup of tea and take his seat in front of the fireplace. I'm alive and well thanks to my alters, who gave me what I needed at the right times. I'm not a collection of fractured pieces. I am Emma.

Now I'm writing the rest of my story.

THE END

AUTHORS NOTE

This book is entirely a work of fiction, but the setting was inspired by The Devil's Thumb Resort in Colorado. If you visit, you'll find gorgeous mountain scenery, a magnificent stone fireplace in the main restaurant, the outdoor hot tub, the little movie theater, the trails, the horses, a spa with specialty tea and a yoga studio with mountain views on three sides. They also have s'mores packets available for roasting marshmallows at the gas firepits. I enjoyed a winter skiing vacation there. I hope I captured some of its beauty for you.

ALSO BY JENIFER RUFF

JENIFER RUFF

USA Today bestselling author Jenifer Ruff writes suspense novels, including the award-winning Agent Victoria Thriller Series. Jenifer lives in North Carolina and Virginia with her family and a pack of greyhounds. If she's not writing, she's probably exploring trails with her dogs. For more information you can visit her website at Jenruff.com

a   amazon.com/stores/author/B00NFZQOLQ

f   facebook.com/authorjruff

O   instagram.com/author.jenifer.ruff/

♪   tiktok.com/@jeniferruff.author

BB   http://bookbub.com/authors/jenifer-ruff

Made in United States
Orlando, FL
15 July 2025

62976802R00163